SUNGOLD

As Danny Murphy drives from Buffalo to her cousin's farm in Minnesota, she hopes to find inspiration for her latest magazine article on farming in the Midwest. When her car breaks down in a Minnesota sunflower field, she finds what she's been looking for in Andrew Drake. For several wonderful days, Danny learns the pleasures of rural life — and life with Andrew. But Andrew wants to be more than just Danny's 'research'. How can she convince him that she doesn't want to simply drive off and leave him?

Books by Jillian Dagg
in the Linford Romance Library:

THE FLETCHER LEGACY

JILLIAN DAGG

SUNGOLD

Complete and Unabridged

LINFORD
Leicester

First published in the
United States of America

First Linford Edition
published 2004

British Library CIP Data

Dagg, Jillian
    Sungold.—Large print ed.—
    Linford romance library
    1. Farming—Minnesota—Fiction
    2. Love stories
    3. Large type books
    I. Title
    813.5′4 [F]

    ISBN 1–84395–564–4

Published by
F. A. Thorpe (Publishing)
Anstey, Leicestershire

Set by Words & Graphics Ltd.
Anstey, Leicestershire
Printed and bound in Great Britain by
T. J. International Ltd., Padstow, Cornwall

This book is printed on acid-free paper

To the memory of my grandmother,
Violet Sankey

1

Crickets and grasshoppers chirped happily in the long grasses beside the road where Danielle Murphy drove. Fields of golden-yellow sunflowers, their round mahogany faces soaking up the bright sun, stretched to a blue horizon. Danny had never seen so many giant flowers all in one place, and they fascinated her.

She slowed the red Trans Am to look, to wonder how she could incorporate the sunflowers into the magazine article she had been commissioned to write. *Earth Now* used hard-hitting writing, not flowery prose, so the glowing descriptions filling her mind made her grin.

Then, above the serenity of the country sounds, Danny heard a bang. The car lurched, and she saw a cloud of murky black smoke curling from the tail pipe. As the car was still moving, she steered it off the highway into a gravel side road. The engine had died, but she tried it again, just for luck.

Nothing. Dead.

Heat swirled around her as she stepped from the car. The warm wind that rushed through her long brown hair and over the horizontal Minnesota fields accentuated a lack of moisture. Danny licked dry lips, wishing for something to drink. Other days she had brought along a full thermos and a picnic lunch, but this morning, as she planned on arriving at her cousin's house around noon, she had eaten a quick breakfast at the motel coffee shop and decided that if she did need extra sustenance, she could stop at another restaurant. She hadn't stopped and wished she had. Then she wouldn't feel thirsty.

She looked at the car and the trails of smoke dancing, taunting her, into the atmosphere. The Trans Am had never let her down before. Or her brother, the previous owner. Of course, she had never driven it all the way from New York to Minnesota before, either. That might have some bearing on why it broke down. But the mechanic at her local service station had told her that although the car was old, it still had a lot of miles left in it. She'd certainly never have it serviced there again.

The sunflowers seemed to be smiling, as if they found her predicament humorous. *Which is fine for you,* she thought. *All you have to do all day is sunbathe and photosynthesize. I could wilt out here.*

Her canvas slip-on shoes crunching over the sand-colored gravel, Danny walked the slight incline to the main road. There was no traffic. That was the beauty of parts of Minnesota — there wasn't any traffic, especially on roads like this highway south of the Canadian border, that would have led her to her cousin's home if her car had held on for a few more miles.

She returned to the Trans Am and touched the hood cautiously. It burned her fingers. Whether the hood was hot from the sun or from the breakdown, she wasn't sure. Maybe the engine had only overheated. She should try starting the car one more time. Sitting in the seat, she turned the key, her teeth clenched with hope. All she produced was a crunching noise that sounded very ominous.

She stood beside the car, the sun scorching her arms and legs, as she was wearing denim walking shorts and a white sleeveless cotton top. She began to analyze her situation. Cultivated fields meant a farm. A farm meant a house. A house meant a telephone. A telephone meant she could phone Doug and Carolyn and let them know of her predicament. She couldn't be far from their house.

She strained her eyes in the brilliant sunshine to a distant clump of trees outlined by a wavering haze of heat. Was there a house behind those trees? Was it worth walking in this heat?

A loud honk broke the pastoral

stillness of nature, and Danny winced. Honking horns reminded her of home, the location of her townhouse near a busy intersection. She hadn't realized how much she had been relishing the country silence until that moment.

'Broken down?' a voice drawled from the cab of a dusty, blue pickup.

Danny said, 'No. I'm just standing around on the side of the road for my health.' Then she smiled, feeling she needed to make an impression because the suntanned face shaded by dark glasses and a green John Deere cap might be the best thing — if she discounted the sunflowers — that she would see all day.

The man chuckled. 'You're on my property, you know.'

'I didn't know that. But when the car began to go wrong, I managed to drive off the road.'

'Won't it start?'

'I don't know.' She fluttered her lashes dramatically. 'I wouldn't think to try.'

He chuckled again. 'Okay, I get your message. This is a major breakdown.'

Danny nodded and watched his descent from the truck. Dusty, black tooled-leather cowboy boots appeared first, followed by long legs in bootcut denims, then narrow hips and waist surrounded by a worn leather belt. His blue shirt hugged a muscular chest. Most of his face was hidden by the sunglasses and cap, but he had a nice mouth that had already smiled a lot.

He prowled over to her dead car, his boots crunching on the gravel. As he bent to open the hood, Danny saw sun-gold hair peeping from beneath the back of his hat. She walked to his side and looked at the engine with him. Not knowing much about engines, she couldn't see a problem.

'What happened?' he asked.

'The car lurched and made a loud bang.'

'Smoke?'

After a few days in Minnesota, Danny had already determined that some of the men were lean with their conversation. She decided to match the leanness. She nodded. 'Black.'

He wriggled a few things around. 'Where're you from?'

'Buffalo, New York.'

'Buffalo, New York. Long way from home.'

'That I am. Do you know what's wrong?'

He looked up and grinned, white teeth flashing in the sun. 'I figure you might have blown your engine.'

'Oh, no!'

'Oh, yes. And it could be a problem. The nearest town big enough to handle this is Pinedale, which is close to thirty miles away. What I'll do is look at it for you. I've done some car repairs in my time. In fact, I worked at a garage when I was a kid, and I really loved the work, but . . . '

'But what?'

'My father died, left me the farm, and that became my priority.'

'These sunflowers?'

He nodded. 'So, do you want me to look at it?'

'Well, I don't want to put you out. All you have to do is let me use your telephone. I'll phone my cousin, and he can come for me.'

'Who's your cousin?'

'Doug Cannon. Do you know him?' Danny figured he probably did.

'Yep. He's my business partner. His wife, Carolyn, is my accountant. Now that I come to think of it, they did mention a relative might be passing through in a day or two.' He extended his hand. 'My name's Andrew Drake.'

'Danielle Murphy,' she said, shaking his warm, slightly roughened hand. 'You can call me Danny.'

She felt relieved that this man wasn't a true stranger, even if she had never met Doug, his wife, or their two boys. When she heard about the article, she had located their address on a Christmas card and had written to them, asking if she could visit. They'd said, yes, of course, they'd love to see her. 'I guess I'm not too far from Doug's place,' she said.

'About a twenty-minute drive if you go the long way, which is the way you were traveling. Ten minutes on the shortcut through the fields. Let me look at the car for you. It might be something easy I can deal with and set you on your way. We can call Doug and let him know you're here. If your car can't be fixed, then I'll take you over there. What I'll do is tow your car up to my house with my truck because it's closer than going to Doug's on a tow.'

'What is required if it *is* a blown engine?' Danny asked as Andrew walked back to the truck.

'Either a rebuild or a reconditioned engine, depending on what's wrong. We'll have to get the parts, of course. It could take a while.'

'What's a while?'

'A few days. A week.'

'Oh, dear, I didn't plan to stay that long,' she said.

'We'll look at it first. I'm merely

giving you the worst scenario. Well, the worst is that the parts could take longer getting here, and then you have to add time for labor. At least it's a domestic make. The parts will be easier to get. Also it's an older model, which means there might be something around here.'

'And it could be something minor.'

'It could be.' He climbed into the truck, started the engine, and drove the pickup around her car. Dust clouded and settled. He parked the truck in front of the Trans Am. Then he climbed out and hauled a chain from the back of the truck.

As he connected the chain, Danny asked, 'Have you always lived around here, Andrew?'

'Always.'

'I'm presuming you were born on the farm.'

'Right on.'

'I've never seen such huge flowers before.'

'We'll have a good harvest this year.'

'That's nice to know when a lot of

farms are dying.'

'Yep.'

He straightened after connecting the chain. 'Okay. You'll have to sit in your car and steer. My house is in that clump of trees. It's not far.'

'Not by Minnesota standards,' Danny murmured.

Andrew laughed. 'Things happen to be spread out around here.'

'You can say that again. But don't.'

Danny got into the Trans Am and closed the door. Andrew got into the pickup. Danny saw him look at her through his rearview mirror before he started the truck engine. His stare gave her a funny feeling in her stomach, and her hand shook as she slipped the gear into neutral. She steered the car as Andrew's truck led her slowly along the dusty road between two fields of sunflowers. She was glad she hadn't attempted to walk the distance. She would have melted. It was much farther than it appeared from the road.

Eventually they reached the copse of

thick-trunked elms and oaks that looked as if they were originally planted as a weather break. Now they were a point of beauty. The two-story house had been structurally patched up over the years. New siding flashed white against peeling white paint around the windows. The brick-red roof shingles seemed to be a recent addition; so did the brick chimney. Pink and white hollyhocks and a few stray sunflowers, their limp faces looking sad as if they'd been kept home from the party out in the fields, straggled up the side of the house.

Andrew towed the Trans Am up the gravel driveway and stopped in front of a garage door. Danny turned the key off, geared to park, and left her car.

'It's beautifully cool here,' she said.

Andrew began to unhitch her car. 'The lake out back helps keep it cool.'

'One of the ten thousand that Minnesota boasts?'

'Nah. This is a little swimming hole.

We named it Sunflower Lake.'

'A perfect name.'

He dumped the chain back in his pickup. 'Do you want a drink or anything before I look at your car?'

'Will your wife mind?'

'I'm not married.'

Did she sense bitterness? Did he want to be married? Had he planned on being married? Had it fallen through? Danny had to admit Andrew Drake fascinated her.

'Have you ever been married?' she asked.

'No. What about you?'

'No.'

'Which evens us out, doesn't it? Come in for a drink. It's a hot day; you're likely parched.'

The wooden porch steps creaked as Danny followed Andrew, the noise accompanying the barking of a dog on the other side of the door. A red-and-blue handwoven rug covered the veranda floor, and a rocking chair had a stars-and-stripes knitted blanket thrown over it. To Danny the porch looked very much Middle America. She loved it and stored the description to use in her article.

The screen door twanged. The oak front door wasn't locked. A black-and-white dog bounded at them, barking at Danny.

'Down, Sadie,' Andrew said, 'This is Danny Murphy. Her car broke down. The pool of marmalade fur on the hearth is Rolfe.'

Danny patted Sadie's head. 'Hi, Sadie. Hi, Rolfe.'

The cat blinked.

'It's too hot for Rolfe,' Andrew explained.

Danny laughed. But her laughter caught in her throat as Andrew removed his hat and dark glasses. His hair was silky gold, his eyes as blue as the Minnesota sky.

He gazed at her for a moment, in the same steady way he'd gazed at her through his rearview mirror earlier. It made her feel unsteady.

Then he turned away. 'What do you like to drink?'

'Anything's fine.'

'Lemonade?'

'Delicious.'

'Make yourself at home,' he said, and with Sadie following at his heels, went through to the kitchen.

Danny wasn't quite relaxed enough to make herself completely at home. She thought her restlessness had something to do with Andrew. So she turned her attention to the house interior. Handwoven rugs, like the one on the porch, covered the polished wood floor. A brick fireplace was faced by two well-worn brown leather armchairs. A sofa, striped orange and brown, dominated one wall. Bookshelves lined another wall. There was also a TV, VCR, and CD player — all appearing a little out of place in the predominantly old-fashioned but peaceful-feeling home.

On the walls the paintings were watercolors of the local landscape —

lakes and prairies. One large painting of sunflowers smiled down on Rolfe, who stretched luxuriously and studied Danny curiously from round green eyes. Stairs, carpeted in a deep orange-red that matched the curtains, led to the top floor.

Danny loved it.

Andrew returned with two glasses of iced lemonade and a plate of what looked like homemade oatmeal cookies.

'Did you bake these?' she asked.

'Not these. They're from the local bakery. Sit down, make yourself comfortable.'

Danny sat down on the sofa with her glass of lemonade and a cookie. 'This is really kind of you, Andrew.'

He perched a few feet from her. 'Do you want the truth?'

She paused in a bite of cookie. 'Okay.'

'I've always wanted the chance to work on a Trans Am like the one you have.'

'You and a hundred other guys. I'm

often getting stopped and asked about it. It was my brother's car.'

'What's he got now?'

'Nothing. He's dead.'

The brass windup clock over the fireplace ticked. Sadie barked outside. Rolfe's paws pattered over the polished floor.

'Don't talk about it if you don't want to,' Andrew said.

'It was an industrial accident. He worked in a factory. A fluke. Four years ago now.'

'Was he your age?'

'Five years older. I'm the baby in the family.'

'Then you have more brothers?'

'Two sisters. How about you?'

'I was the only child, which is why I'm working the farm. If there had been someone else to leave it to, Dad would have. He knew I wasn't particularly interested.'

'But you look at home here.'

'It *is* home. Don't get me wrong. It's just that it's . . . '

Lonely, Danny added to herself. *He's lonely. He lives all the way out here on his own with only his TV, VCR, CD player, dog, and cat for company. He's very lonely.*

Andrew got to his feet and said, 'Yeah, that's it,' as if she spoke aloud, as if he knew what she was thinking. As if they were thinking the same thing. 'Anyway, I'll take a look at your car.' He paused. 'Do you want to wait to phone Doug until after I've diagnosed your problem?'

'Yes. That's the best thing to do. I don't want to alarm them. I talked to them last night from near Thief River Falls.' She stood up. 'Thank you for your help.'

Andrew walked to the table, picked up his hat and sunglasses. 'Thank me when I achieve results.'

Danny watched him leave. She heard Sadie bark for Andrew; Rolfe left the living room. She finished her lemonade and cookies and then walked into the kitchen with her empty glass and plate.

Sparkling clean was her first impression. Eclectic was her second. The gas stove was old; the fridge was new. The countertops were a marble mottled Formica, a bit chewed and stained in places by years of having hot pots put on them or being accidentally scarred by knives. The gray linoleum floor was polished, and the pine table and chairs were large and serviceable. The sink was white porcelain, and there were dishes drying in a pink plastic drainer. She rinsed her glass and plate and added them to the drainer. From the window, through some birch trees, she saw the sparkle of water ... likely Sunflower Lake.

She didn't feel like snooping upstairs. Instead, she went outside and walked over to Andrew.

'How's it going?'

Andrew grabbed a rag to wipe his greasy hands. 'The good news: It's fixable. The bad news: It *is* the engine.'

'Then it's going to take a while?'

'Yep. I'll get on the phone to the

service station in Pinedale to see what they've got. They might have a reconditioned engine they can pick up from somewhere close by that we can scavenge for parts or even use to replace this one.'

'I'll have to repay you for all this work.'

'We'll worry about that when the time comes. Let's go give Carolyn and Doug a call.'

Doug was out when they called. Carolyn spoke to Andrew, then Danny. She was sorry about the car but pleased that Danny ran into Andrew for help. Andrew loaded Danny's two bulky bags, one that was heavy because it contained her portable computer, into the back of the pickup to drive her to Doug and Carolyn's house. They drove along dusty roads lined with fields of sunflowers and corn.

'You grow corn as well as flowers here,' Danny said, wishing she had her tape recorder or her notebook available to make some notes. Andrew could give her some new perspective for her article.

'As corn and sunflowers are both intertilled crops, they can be harvested the same way,' he said. 'Intertilled means the crop is planted in rows and we cultivated between the rows. You can pretty well rest assured that if corn grows, then sunflowers will grow.'

'When do you plant the flowers?'

'After last frost.'

'When's that out here?'

'For northern Minnesota it's around May twenty-fifth. We like to get the seeds in the ground ASAP after that date. First frost is around September fifteenth.'

Danny smiled. 'In this heat, frost seems impossible, even tempting.'

'And we get too much of that as well. Winter's vicious around these parts. Twenty, thirty, sometimes even forty below.'

Danny shivered. 'That cools me down thinking about it. How do you water your fields?'

'Sunflowers are pretty hardy. They don't need much water and hardly any cultivation once they're in the sunshine. This summer's been perfect.'

'How tall do they grow?'

'Oh, anywhere from three to twenty feet. Most of mine run around four or five feet, which makes for easier harvesting.'

'Do you have to plant them each year?'

'Yep. Helianthus annus. Although some flowers, if they're let to seed, will return as perennials.'

'You don't let them seed?'

'No. Most of our seeds go for oil, poultry feed, and packaged seeds.'

'When my brother was a kid, he used to call sunflower seeds, skunk seeds,' Danny told him. 'He loved them. I think he got addicted when he visited an uncle who used to live in Minneapolis. That was Doug's father's brother.'

Andrew chuckled. 'Do you have a lot of relatives in these parts?'

'No. That uncle lives in California now. Only Doug and his family, whom I've never met. They're all relatives on my mother's side. Doug's a cousin. Mainly I'm here to do some research. I'm a journalist, and I'm doing an article on the current state of our farms for *Earth Now* magazine. Do you know it?'

'Can't say I do. I don't have time to read many magazines. Do you work for it?'

'No. I free-lance. But it is one of my regular magazines. New York State isn't all buildings. There's a great deal of lovely countryside and farms.'

'Then why don't you do your article on those farms?'

'Because I've done articles on those farms. I felt like seeing another part of the country to get a slant on all the problems we hear about. So much of our farmland is disappearing.'

'Middle America,' Andrew said and jerked the truck over a pothole.

Danny felt her throat tighten slightly

at his tone. Had she sounded derogatory?

'If my father hadn't died when he had, this place would have gone to wrack and ruin. It was already on its way out of the system.'

'That's the type of thing I want to know. Would you sit down and talk to me? Use a tape recorder, maybe?'

'I don't know. I'll think about it.'

'I don't want to abuse your hospitality,' Danny said. 'I mean, you've been very kind about my car.'

Andrew looked at her. 'I have this impression you feel that you've hit a winner with me.'

'I knew Doug worked on a farm, but I have to admit I didn't expect to meet a real farmer at such close quarters.'

'A real farmer. Huh!'

He did think she was putting him down in some way. She didn't want to upset him, especially when she was going to be indebted to him enough for fixing her car and helping her out. She said softly, 'I find you interesting.'

'Because I'm a farmer and handy for your article.'

Oh, no, she had really put her foot in it. What did her brother Len used to call her? 'Candy-coated-foot Danny' because she was always putting her foot in her mouth. He figured it had to be candy-coated to be that addictive.

'My car didn't break down on purpose,' she said.

'Lucky it did though, huh?'

She didn't want to argue with him. 'Look, Andrew, I would have met you, anyway, as I'm staying with Doug for a few days. Let's forget about the article. Forget I mentioned it. I'll do it my own way without your help. I already have a disk full of notes on my computer. I just thought that your perspective could add luster to it, authenticity.'

'What you have to realize,' he said, 'is that farmers aren't hicks. We're educated men. I have degrees in business and agriculture.'

'I never expected anything different. You also have to realize that journalists aren't muckrakers. I have degrees in journalism and English literature.'

So there, she thought.

Carolyn and Doug lived in a big family house with dove-gray siding. A maroon minivan and a silver truck with a white cab were parked outside. Andrew stopped his truck alongside them. A couple in their mid-thirties were sitting on the neat white porch. They both ran down the steps when they saw Andrew's truck.

Doug was a broad-shouldered, dark-haired man with a spiky, tickly-looking moustache. He looked a little like Danny's brother, Len. Carolyn was very small, slim, tanned, in white shorts and top. Her hair was a mane of jet-black splendor. They both hugged Danny warmly as if they saw her all the time.

Doug and Andrew dealt with her luggage, and Carolyn ushered Danny around the side of the house to the patio beside the pool. When Doug and Andrew appeared, Carolyn served iced tea with sprigs of home-grown mint dangling on the rims of the glasses.

Carolyn said to Andrew, 'Danny's probably told you she's a journalist. She's writing an article for a magazine. She's in Minnesota doing research.'

'Yes. She mentioned it.' Andrew leaned down to pet the black cat rubbing his chair leg.

'Andrew isn't too happy with me,' Danny explained. 'I made him sound as if a farmer were something curious I wanted to examine.'

'Andrew, don't be like that,' Carolyn said. 'Let me tell you, Danny, Andrew has done wonders with this farm. It was really run-down, and now it's . . . flowering.' She smiled.

'I think I had a hand in it as well,' Doug commented.

'Oh, yes, dear, of course,' Carolyn said.

Doug smiled at Danny. 'You see where I stand in this household? Under the thumb of the accountant. This farm is run by our accountant, Danny. You can mention that in your article.'

Danny smiled. She liked Doug. He seemed less complicated than Andrew. Of course, he was a relative. Andrew was just a . . . man. She knew she had a chance for good interviews from her relatives. Yet it was Andrew who intrigued her the most.

Andrew left after he finished his iced tea. He said he'd phone later and report on her car when he'd talked to the Pinedale Service Center.

Danny walked him to his truck on the gravel driveway. Gravel seemed to be standard here. Too much land to pave, she supposed, far too expensive.

'Don't let the car repairs hold you up from the farm work,' she said. 'And if you need to purchase any parts, I'll use my credit card.'

'I'll deal with it and let you know,' he told her. 'Don't worry.'

'Thanks for everything,' she said.

He climbed into the truck, started the engine, reversed, and left with a silent salute.

Danny walked into the air-conditioned house, and Carolyn showed her to a pleasant blue-and-white bedroom overlooking the pool. Her luggage was already beside the bed. From the window she could see the chimney of Andrew's house peeking through the cluster of trees.

As she fussed with straightening the blue, flowered comforter, Carolyn said, 'Andrew seems to have taken quite a shine to you.'

Danny felt her cheeks flush. 'Oh, no. He got stuck with me because I steered my broken-down car onto his property.'

'And he'd help out, that's for sure. He's a sweet man — pure gold, I'll tell you that. All he needs is a nice woman to fall in love with and marry.'

'Doesn't he have a girlfriend?'

'No. I'm not saying that a lot of the local women haven't tried to be his girlfriend, but he doesn't bite to their advances. A few years ago he met someone. She wasn't from around here.

When she went home to Boston, I think he was pretty hurt. He hasn't come to the local dances since. There's one this Friday — we should drag him along with you.'

'Why me? I'm going home to Buffalo when my car's fixed.'

'I suppose.' Carolyn looked disappointed. Obviously she was trying hard to match Andrew up. 'You'll enjoy the dance, anyway. You'll be able to talk to some of the other farmers for your article.'

'It sounds like fun. We'll see how it goes with the car. That regulates how long I'll be here. I don't want to put you out, Carolyn.'

'You're not putting me out. I've been excited to know you're coming. Here I am, stuck out here with two boys for children, a husband, and a male boss. Even the two cats are male. I'm desperate for female company.'

Danny grinned. 'Andrew's dog is female.'

'I forgot about old Sadie. Still, she's

not on my side. She dotes on Andrew. You can barely peel her away from him. Anyway, I'll let you get settled while I go and start dinner. Don't worry about helping or anything. I'm pleased to have company. Doug's going into Pinedale to a meeting tonight. We'll be able to have a good chat.'

When she was alone, Danny placed her computer on the small table near the window as it was close to an electrical outlet. She quickly typed in as much as she could remember about growing sunflowers and added a few extra notes of her own observations, especially the description of Andrew's front porch. She also set up her tape recorder, ready for Carolyn and Doug if they felt like talking when they had a spare moment. Danny wasn't going to rush them. She was sure she had at least a week here, and the way Carolyn spoke, she could stay longer if she wanted.

After getting permission from Carolyn to use the phone on her telephone credit card, Danny called her editor at *Earth Now* to fill her in on her whereabouts. Gina Bernstein had bought Danny's first article and had used everything ever since. It was a rare jewel to get an editor who loved everything a writer wrote, and it hadn't been difficult to make friends with Gina when they finally met face-to-face. However, she didn't tell Gina about Andrew.

The phone rang after she hung up with Gina, and she picked it up.

'Carolyn?' a male voice asked.

'No. I'll get her.'

'Is this Danny?'

'Yes.'

'It's Andrew. It's you I wanted to talk to, anyway. I spoke to the Pinedale Service Center. No problem in getting you either a reconditioned engine or parts. But either way it's a week.'

'I don't believe I have much choice,' she said. 'Thanks for your trouble.'

'No trouble. Be seeing you.'

As she hung up the phone, Danny

wondered if her reticence to tell Gina about Andrew was because he was such an attractive man who affected her feelings.

2

Carolyn and Doug's kitchen was high-tech compared to Andrew's, with a microwave, a dishwasher, a built-in oven, a countertop stove, an island with a sink in the middle for washing vegetables, and a separate dining area with a round white table and chairs with blue cushions. There were blue-and-white curtains at the windows and a skylight in the ceiling. With white counters, it was bright, modern, and cheery.

Carolyn handed Danny a can of pop and made her sit down at the table. Meanwhile Carolyn whipped up a huge meal of roast beef, vegetables, potatoes, and salad.

'You don't have to cook such a big meal,' Danny said, feeling useless sitting at the table while Carolyn worked. But she wouldn't let her help.

'I planned it for your arrival. It's no trouble.'

'It's kind of you.'

'You're a relative.' Carolyn placed a glass bowl of salad on the table. 'It's not often we get relatives to stay. It's just unfortunate for you that your car broke down. Although if it means I can have you here longer, then I'm going to be selfish.'

Carolyn reminded Danny of her oldest sister, Sue, a down-to-earth homemaker with three kids and a husband. Rita, on the other hand, was a high-powered career woman, a finance whiz, never married. Danny figured she fitted somewhere in between the two.

Doug entered the kitchen, dressed in slacks and an open-neck short-sleeved shirt. He selected a piece of lettuce from the salad and munched.

'Will you have time for dinner?' his wife asked.

'No. It's a dinner meeting. What I need, though, is energy to drive there. I'll make a sandwich.'

'I'll make you one. Sit down and talk to your cousin.'

Doug did as he was told. Smiling, he said to Danny, 'She's proving who runs this institution, isn't she?' He leaned closer to her and peered at her. 'Yeah, you're from the Cannon clan, all right. Hazel eyes and a no-nonsense nose.'

'Doug, don't insult Danny,' Carolyn said. 'She's pretty.'

'She's pretty, that's for sure, but not in an insipid way — the strong Cannon way.'

Carolyn placed a sandwich on a plate in front of him. 'Danny, don't let him tease you.'

'I don't mind his teasing.' Danny had been teased all her life by Len. She missed the fun.

Doug finished his sandwich and slotted the plate in the dishwasher, with a comment to say he'd been trained to do that. Then he lifted his truck keys off the hook by the back door and kissed Carolyn's neck. 'Miss you, love. I won't be too late. Enjoy yourself, Danny.'

'I will. Thanks for everything, Doug.'

'Andrew's done it all so far,' he said. 'See you ladies later.'

After Doug's truck engine was out of hearing range, Danny heard different sounds — the whir of bicycle wheels, boys' voices, a dog barking.

'The crew's home,' Carolyn said and went to the screen door. She called out, 'Okay, guys, we have a guest, so no funny business. What have you got there?'

'Fish,' boys' voices said.

'Oh, no. Well, I'm not touching them. Keep them for your father.'

Two boys entered the kitchen, one carrying a covered pail. They both wore jeans, shirts, and scuffed white sneakers and had dark hair and smooth tans that were the product of a long outdoor summer. They looked like Carolyn.

With a wave of her hand, Carolyn noted who each boy was as she said, 'Kyle, Sean, this is Danny Murphy, your father's cousin from New York.'

'Hi,' Kyle said.

'Hi,' Sean said.

'Have you been to Yankee Stadium?'

'The Empire State Building?'

'Central Park?'

'Macy's?'

Their mother said, 'She's from Buffalo, boys; that's the other side of the state.'

'What's the difference?' Kyle asked.

'There's a lot of difference, stupid,' Sean said, suddenly making sense of the distance. 'Haven't you heard of the Buffalo Bills?'

'I'm not the only one who's stupid, stupid. You thought she came from New York.'

Danny smiled. 'I have been to New York City. And I have been up the Empire State Building. However, I live closer to Niagara Falls.'

'Niagara Falls. Wow! Guys go over the falls in barrels, don't they?'

'Enough,' Carolyn said. 'Go wash up. Your father's at a meeting tonight; he'll be home later. And put those fish in a corner somewhere, Kyle. Where's Toad?'

'Outside. Do you want him in?'

'No. Leave him out. You can feed him later.'

'Who's Toad?' Danny asked.

'The dog,' Carolyn said, moving the pail Kyle put in the middle of the kitchen away from her immediate vicinity. 'One thing I cannot do,' she explained, 'is gut fish.'

The two cats, black-and-white Panda and pure-black Thunder, stalked the scent of the fish. Panda sniffed. Thunder tried to figure a way to pry the lid off the pail. Panda lay beside the pail, waiting for a fish to escape.

Danny laughed. 'Is it always like this?'

Carolyn nodded. 'Always.'

'Then I'm going to help you,' Danny said. 'Let me set the table.'

The boys returned, smelling of soap but otherwise not looking much different. They obviously had a routine because each went to the fridge and poured a drink to accompany his dinner. Kyle, milk. Sean, juice.

'Pour something for Danny,' Carolyn said.

'I'm fine. I still have some pop left.'

'Sure?'

'Sure, I'm sure.'

'Then we'll eat. Sit.'

Danny hid a chuckle. Carolyn treated her boys like dogs.

'Do you want to go fishing with us one day?' Kyle asked Danny as they ate.

'That might be fun,' she said. 'Where do you fish?'

'Sunflower Creek. It's a little creek that runs off the lake. We're not allowed to go to the lake without Dad.'

'But if she came,' Sean piped up, 'we could probably go.'

'Boys,' Carolyn interrupted, 'Danny's here working. Although she might stay a little longer because her car broke down.'

'What happened?' Kyle asked.

'The engine blew up.'

'Blew up?' Sean said.

Danny nodded. 'Black smoke, the whole bit.'

'And luckily Uncle Andy came along with his truck and gave her a tow,' Carolyn said.

'So what's going to happen to your engine?' Sean asked.

'Andrew's going to fix it,' Danny told him.

'What type of car?'

'A Trans Am.'

'Finished?' their mother asked them.

'Yes.'

'Then go play, feed Toad, and leave Danny in peace.'

'And leave me in peace,' Carolyn muttered when her sons were gone, the screen on the back door still zinging from their slam. A dog barked excitedly. She poured coffee from a glass carafe into two blue mugs. 'Do you want to take this outside or stay in the cool for a while?'

'We can stay here and clear away the dishes,' Danny said. 'And you're not going to tell me not to help, because that's ridiculous.'

Coffee drunk, dishes in the dishwasher, kitchen tidied, they went outside to sit on the patio. Beneath the late-day hot sun, the blue pool sparkled. Beyond the pool was a lawn and an attempt at flower beds around it. A small vegetable garden was laid in strips before the property dissolved into a wood lot.

While they sat, Carolyn told Danny a bit about herself. The company her brother Mac worked for had transferred him to California a few years ago. Her mom and her dad, who was retired from farm-machinery sales, had joined him and his family in San Diego last year. Her brother and his wife had two children. Doug, Carolyn, and the kids planned a trip to visit.

'Do you miss them?' Danny asked.

'Occasionally at family events. But most of the time we're so busy here and it's so hectic that there isn't time to worry about it.'

They'd lapsed into a friendly silence

by the time Doug returned from his meeting. He poured himself a nightcap bottle of beer and sat out with the women.

'Cousin Danny,' he said. 'Your mother is my father's cousin? Right?'

'Right. I think,' Danny said. 'I've never gotten it completely straight. Families are pretty vague most of the time about who's who. Are your parents still around?'

'Heavens, yes. We'll have them over Saturday evening for a barbecue. How does that sound, love?'

'Fine with me,' Carolyn said. 'Marcia as well.'

'If she wants to come.'

'Who's Marcia?' Danny asked.

'Doug's sister. She never married. She's a schoolteacher and not that sociable. You have to drag her to family get-togethers most of the time.'

'I'd like to meet her,' Danny said. 'It's fun discovering new relatives.'

Danny went with the Cannon family for their nightly stroll, along with Toad, a small, determined black, brown, and white hound. The boys ran in and out of sunflower fields with Toad at their heels, puffing to keep up. Doug, Carolyn, and Danny walked leisurely in the warm evening air.

Andrew's truck came the opposite way. When he saw them, he stopped in the middle of the road and leaned out the window. 'How's it going?'

'Fine,' everyone said.

'Danny settling in?'

'Sure am,' she told him.

'Great. See you all tomorrow.'

'Good night, Andrew,' Carolyn said as he drove off, leaving a dust cloud.

When they returned home, the boys went to bed and Danny followed their exodus. It had been a long, somewhat frustrating, yet exciting day.

★ ★ ★

Splash.
  Bark.
  Splash.

Bark.

Splash. Splash.

Bark. Bark.

'Boys! Toad!' Carolyn shouted. 'You'll wake Danny.'

Danny slipped out of bed and into her easily packed cotton robe. She peeped out the window. Under brilliant morning sunshine Sean and Kyle were in the pool, volleying a red-and-green beach ball to each other. The tiles surrounding the pool dripped. Soggy towels were dumped in heaps. Toad pattered around the edge of the pool, refereeing the action.

Carolyn, dressed in jeans and a shirt, her hair in a ponytail, ran out of the house and shook one of the towels.

'Oh, you two, what do you do with your towels, try to drown them? Come on in now. Breakfast is ready. I'm going into town this morning, and we've got a guest.'

Danny hoped the reference to the guest didn't mean she was too much added work for Carolyn, who seemed to have her fair share of jobs. She quickly showered and dressed in white shorts and a bright-pink T-shirt. She left her hair damp to dry naturally and hurried downstairs. The kitchen rocked with chatter and action and smelled of coffee and toast.

'Hi,' Carolyn said when she saw Danny. 'I hope these guys didn't wake you.'

'No. I was already awake.' In fact, she'd heard a vehicle leave early — probably Doug's, as he didn't seem to be around. 'I should be up helping anyway.'

'No way. As soon as they've gone fishing for the day, we can relax and eat our breakfast on the patio. Do you want a swim?'

'Maybe later,' Danny said. 'Are you sure you don't want help?'

'I'll ask when I do. At the moment, relax, and I mean it. I deal with this confusion each and every day of my life. Pour yourself some coffee or juice and go out back. I'll join you soon. I'm driving into town. Do you want to come?'

'Sure, but — '

'I want female company, remember. I *desire* it.' Carolyn made a face. '*Boys*. Men never grow up, so we can categorize them all together. Have you finished, Kyle, Sean?'

'Yep,' they chorused.

'Okay. Get dressed and out of here in ten flat.'

Adhering to Carolyn's instructions, Danny poured herself orange juice from a decanter on the table and went outside into the sunshine. She placed her glass on the umbrella table and walked to the pool edge. Kneeling, she reached into the water to feel the temperature. It was lukewarm. Gorgeous. She'd certainly take up the offer of a swim later.

'Hi, there.'

Danny twisted around to see Andrew. Same dusty boots and jeans as yesterday, but today a black shirt was tucked into the worn belt. The black would be a wonderful foil for his golden hair, if it weren't jammed beneath his green hat. His eyes were covered by his dark glasses.

'Hi, there,' she said, standing up. 'How's it going?'

'Your car's in my garage. I've looked at the engine, and it seems that it's either a cracked head, piston rod, or a major valve job. It might be all three. I'd say go for an entire engine.'

'Is that expensive?'

'Don't worry about how much it costs. Consider that I feel it a privilege to work on a car like that one. It's such a great car, it's worth getting fixed.'

'There's no question about getting it fixed. But I'm going to pay you.'

'Danny,' he said.

By the way he pronounced her name, she knew she shouldn't argue any longer. Nevertheless, she did. 'It's a lot of work for you, Andrew. My being here for longer than I intended is also a lot of work for Carolyn. Are you sure you want to tackle the engine yourself?

Couldn't the service station do it?'

'No. I want to do it,' he said with a certain amount of stubbornness, like a determined kid. 'And I don't want you to be thinking that way about being trouble. Carolyn's tickled you're here.'

'Am I ever!' Carolyn agreed, coming out of the house. 'Want a mug of coffee, Andrew? It's Doug's early A.M. brew.'

'Count me out,' Andrew said, adjusting the peak of his hat lower over his face and making a move to leave.

Danny heard Carolyn give a little sigh of irritation. 'Andrew, are you going to take Danny on a tour of the farm today so she can research her article? She has a splendid opportunity here.'

Seeing Andrew stiffen slightly, Danny inserted, 'It doesn't matter, Carolyn. He's probably busy.'

'Not too busy to give you a short tour. We're going into town, Andrew. We'll be back after lunch. Pick her up then.'

'Is this how you got Doug to marry

you?' Andrew asked.

'Andrew,' Carolyn said, 'Danny's only here for a short time. Well, longer because of the car, which gives her a chance for extra research. She *is* on a working vacation, you know.'

'Yeah, I know.'

And he doesn't like it, Danny thought. 'Forget it,' she said. 'Another day.'

Carolyn made a sound. Andrew shifted from one booted foot to the other. Danny felt caught in the middle.

Andrew cleared his throat. 'Well, another day might be busier.' He glanced at Danny. 'Okay if I drive by here about one-thirty?'

'Terrific.' Danny wondered if it would be prudent of her to take along her tape recorder and notebook. Maybe the notebook alone to start. She would ask Carolyn how to tackle Andrew. Although Carolyn's idea was probably head-on. Did Andrew feel bossed around by his accountant?

'See you then,' he said.

Danny heard his footsteps on the gravel path, then his truck starting up. She looked at Carolyn. 'You forced him to take me?'

'So what?'

Danny laughed. 'You're really bad.'

'Andrew understands me. He's easy-going, really, even though he doesn't give that impression. He won't mind showing you around. He'll probably enjoy it.'

'I hope you're right.'

They ate toast and drank coffee, and then Danny loaded the dishwasher while Carolyn went to change her chlorine-splashed shirt for a fresh one.

Carolyn drove the minivan. Danny perched next to her on the seat, which seemed dramatically elevated compared to the low Trans Am. She asked, 'Do you think Andrew would mind if I took along my notebook or tape recorder this afternoon on the tour of the farm?'

'Under the circumstances, judging by the way he's acting, I wouldn't surprise him with it,' Carolyn said as they bumped to a stop on the slope of a gravel road that met the highway. There was no traffic. Carolyn pressed her foot on the gas, and the van lurched onto the straight highway and gathered speed. 'Make sure it's okay with him. We did rather pressure him into the tour in the first place.'

'Now you admit it.' Danny laughed. 'Anyway, I always have my notebook in my bag.' She patted the canvas tote that served as her purse and hold-all for everything she carried with her.

The drive to Pinedale was along the highway Danny would have driven if her car hadn't broken down at the precise time it did. On either side of the road, fields of sunflowers and green cornstalks grew beneath the sunshine.

'Why did they ever call Pinedale, Pinedale?' Danny remarked. 'Why not Sunflower Dell?'

Carolyn laughed. 'Who knows? Maybe there were more pine trees in that area.'

Were there? Yes. Two on the outskirts

by the town sign. A clump beside a park. Then Danny didn't see another pine tree as Carolyn drove past the service center, where her car would have been repaired if Andrew hadn't come along or been connected to her cousin; past houses in nice neat yards, a motor lodge with a restaurant, a church, a brick high school silent for the summer. There were two banks, two supermarkets, a drugstore, a post office, two fast-food places, a hardware store, a farming implement outlet, another church, and a variety of interesting clothing stores.

Carolyn parked the van by the curb on the main street, and they both got out into the brilliant sunshine.

'I have to go to the bank. Do you have to do anything?'

'Nothing in particular. I'll window-shop.'

'Choose something nice to buy,' Carolyn said and set off to do her business.

Danny window-shopped for a while,

then perched on a concrete planter containing summer flowers. She watched the vehicles drive in and out of town. Most of them were dusty, like Andrew's. Each time she saw a truck that might be Andrew's, her heart flipped.

Carolyn finished in the bank, and they went shopping for clothes, Carolyn hunting bargains, obviously relishing the excuse to shop.

'Doug wants to buy me one of those stickers, *Born to Shop*, for the back of my van,' she said. 'But he hasn't seen one anywhere yet.'

'My neighbor in Buffalo has one. I'll ask her where she got it, and if I can get one, I'll send it to you.'

Carolyn sighed. 'I keep forgetting you're here only temporarily. I want Andrew to get hitched so there will be another woman around.'

'Don't push him too hard,' Danny said. 'And please don't push him on me.'

'Don't you like him?'

'Of course, I like him. But not that way.'

In one shop Danny purchased a T-shirt, thinking she was probably going to run out of clothes with the extra time spent here.

'Do you have something to wear on Friday night?' Carolyn asked her when they were back on the sidewalk.

'Friday night?'

'The dance.'

'I suppose I'll still be here. Will slacks and a blouse do?'

'No dress?'

'I didn't bring one. Every time I pack one, I never wear it. Should I buy one?'

'Why don't we both buy one?' Carolyn said. 'There's this lovely little dress store that just opened up, and I've been dying for an excuse to buy something there.'

The dress store was full of pretty cotton sun-dresses. Carolyn purchased a white one, with lace edging the V neckline and the hem. White looked stunning with her black hair. Danny chose a rose-pink dress with a full skirt, nipped-in waist, square neckline, and straps. She imagined herself in it, dancing with Andrew.

'Do you think Andrew will go to the dance?' she asked Carolyn after they'd been ushered into a booth at the log-cabin-style restaurant beside the Pinedale Motor Lodge.

'He can't mope over that woman forever,' Carolyn said.

'Do you really think he's still moping over her?'

'Beats me, but he hasn't been exactly outgoing lately. And look how hesitant he is about taking you out.'

'He's hesitant with me because he thinks I'm here to write an article about farming that might put him down. Which isn't true.'

'I'll ask him to the dance.'

'What if he says no?'

'He won't say no if we're all going. He'll know I'll bug him about it forever.'

A waitress came to take their order of

sandwiches. Carolyn introduced Danny as their cousin from Buffalo.

'That's a coincidence,' the waitress said. 'I have a cousin in Buffalo.'

After lunch they stopped at a supermarket for groceries, then drove home. Andrew's dusty blue truck drew up to Carolyn's house at the same time as Carolyn stopped the van. Both women jumped out of the van, and Carolyn opened the side so they could gather their purchases.

'I'll carry the groceries in,' Andrew said, easily handling the two bags.

The women followed him into the cool kitchen.

'We bought dresses for the Friday dance,' Carolyn informed him. 'You're coming, aren't you? To keep Danny company.'

Andrew wasn't wearing either hat or dark glasses, so Danny watched his expression. He didn't show much emotion. But he said, 'Well, if it's planned.'

'It's planned and it's engraved in

stone,' Carolyn declared.

Danny chuckled.

Andrew glanced at her. 'Do you want me to accompany you?'

Put me on the spot, she thought. 'Better than being the odd one out. Three's a crowd and all that. And *yes*, I would like you to accompany me.'

Andrew still didn't show any emotion. 'Fine with me, then. I'll have to dig out my best clothes.'

'He looks like a movie star when he gets dressed up,' Carolyn said as she unloaded the groceries. 'Now you two, get out of my hair. I have to work on the books this afternoon.'

As Andrew and Danny walked out into the hot noon sun, Andrew said, 'She could run your life if you let her.'

'Do you let her?'

'Most of the time it's easier to cave in; otherwise you'll never hear the end of it. She feels responsible for me, I think. Like I'm one of her brood along with Doug and the kids.' Andrew opened the passenger door of his truck.

'Your wagon, ma'am.'

Danny climbed into the seat. Sadie stirred from the back and poked her head over the seats to sniff Danny. Danny patted the dog's jet-black head. 'How are you today?' she asked.

'Woof,' Andrew said as he started the engine.

Danny laughed. His hat and sun-glasses were on a shelf below the dash. Had he left them off for her benefit? Did he consider this a sort of date? Did he like her? Or was he merely being courteous because there was no choice? Carolyn definitely had pressured him.

'I brought my notebook along. Not the tape recorder. I thought we could do that another evening. Maybe with Carolyn and Doug.'

Andrew looked across at her as he drove. 'You're not going to sit beside me and take notes, are you?'

'Not if you don't want me to.'

'I'd rather you didn't.'

'I won't then. The book's in my bag. I'll leave it there.'

'So what do you want to see?' he asked.

'Show me around the farm.'

'Okay.'

Feeling unwanted, Danny sighed.

Andrew drove for a while, then parked the truck on a gravel road edging a sunflower field. Sadie leaped out and pattered off down the dusty road to explore. Danny walked with Andrew up a dirt path between two rows of flowers. She'd never been close to sunflowers before, and she saw that the leaves were coarse, almost heart-shaped.

Andrew flicked some seeds into his palm.

'Skunk seeds,' she said.

'They're not ripe yet. We harvest in the fall. Because the seeds contain high amounts of phosphorus and calcium, they store well without deteriorating. If you take them home and put them in a pan in the oven for a while, they're real good. They keep for a year or more in a jar.'

'What do you do with the plants?'

'Store them in silos and use them for silage. Cattle feed. As we don't have any cattle, we sell it.'

'You're enterprising,' Danny said. 'Do you use chemicals?'

'No. We farm organically. We've experimented with crop and field rotation and planting certain plants that keep the bugs away, and so far it's working. Care has to be taken because sunflowers can contract a gray mold and/or a disease that discolors the stems so they eventually collapse from the inside out.'

'Sounds sad.'

'It is. You have to think of farms as life and achieve that aim.'

'That's an interesting concept.'

'Isn't that what farming's all about?' Andrew said. 'Food for animals and humans, to keep the chain alive.'

'That's why farms can't be allowed to die.'

'I know. You see, some farmers overextended themselves financially with high-tech machinery. Others, closer to cities, have sold out to developers. There's also the global economy that affects us more and more. And other farms have died because the kids don't want to farm and leave.'

'Like you didn't want to,' Danny said as they strolled back to the truck. Sadie chased a butterfly, but the butterfly was quicker than the dog and escaped.

'True. Although, don't get me wrong. I like farming; I like the life. It's in my blood more than I ever thought. And sometimes I wonder if I was being rebellious by not wanting to follow in my father's footsteps. Trouble is, after me there's no one, unless Kyle and Sean want to farm. Right now Kyle wants to be an astronaut and Sean a guitarist in a rock band.'

Danny smiled. 'They'll change their minds. I wanted to be an actress before a writer.'

'When did the writing start?'

'In my teens. I edited and wrote articles for the school newspaper. I supported myself with it during college, so I kept writing after graduation. It was better than a real job.'

'Don't you consider it a real job?'

'I mean, I don't have to be somewhere nine to five or longer. I can take time off if I want.'

'A bit like farming.'

'Probably. Hard work, disappointments, and good times.'

They reached the truck and climbed in, Sadie panting between them. Andrew drove along the road until he came to a rutty grass track. He turned onto the track and drove to a big wooden barn, some storage sheds, and a long, low greenhouse. Behind these buildings were six huge silver cylindrical structures. The area was neat and well kept.

'The cylinders are the storage silos,' he explained. 'I use the greenhouse to experiment with organic growing processes. I guess your magazine deals with that type of thing.'

'They're always looking for articles

on natural farming,' Danny said, leaning her arm over the wound-down window. The air smelled sweet and aromatic, filled with the hypnotic buzz of insects. 'This farm is super, Andrew.'

'I'm pleased you think so,' he said formally. 'Let's see if we can find Doug.'

They drove along gravel roads that ran as far as the eye could see until they spotted the sun winking on Doug's silver truck. Doug, in jeans, shirt, and black Stetson, was in a cornfield, inspecting growth. They left Andrew's truck by the side of the field and spilled out, with Sadie barking and running in Doug's direction. Doug crouched to greet the dog.

When Andrew and Danny reached him, Doug said, 'Hi, there.' He straightened with a stick in his hand and threw it between two rows of corn for Sadie. 'Sorry I took off so early this morning without seeing you, Danny. I'll be home for supper tonight. Not that I have much choice. Carolyn won't cook fish; she's got a thing about the eyes. The boys once put a fish head on her pillow to tease her, except she didn't feel very teased. It scared the what-all out of her.'

Danny laughed. 'I imagine it did. And don't worry about being around for me. I don't want to get in the way.'

Her cousin's moustache made his grin lopsided. 'You're too small for that. So what do you think of the place? Decided to come here and live?' Doug's arm swept the massive cornfield.

'It's really lovely, but I do have a place to live,' she said, noticing that Andrew walked away from them. He bent to check a flourishing cornstalk. She saw him reach out and check on the progress of the cob.

'Do you have a boyfriend?' Doug asked.

'No one steady.'

'Do you have boyfriends?'

'I go on dates sometimes,' Danny said and saw Doug glance over to Andrew. She thought that it was probable her cousin was in league with Carolyn as far as matching Andrew up with a wife. To lure him from the trail, she said, 'I don't have much time for all that as my life is busy with my free-lance writing. One day I want to write a book about some of the subjects of my articles. I've got all sorts of things I want to do.'

'What happens if you fall in love?' Doug asked.

'If it happens, it happens. It hasn't happened yet.'

'Yet,' Doug repeated. Then, as if tiring of the subject, he called out, 'Hey, Andrew, how do you think the Twins are doing this season?'

Andrew and Doug discussed baseball. Danny threw more sticks for Sadie. Her brother, Len, had been a ball fan. Like Kyle and Sean, he had always wanted to see a game at Yankee Stadium. He didn't make it. She wondered if Kyle and Sean ever would.

Every once in a while Andrew glanced her way, and they returned smiles. Eventually he adjusted his dark glasses, touched the peak of his hat, and said, 'We should get a move on. See you later, Doug.'

''Bye, you two. I'll be home early, Danny.'

Andrew drove Danny back to Carolyn's house and let her off. He honked the truck horn in a farewell as he left the house, and she waved to him.

When Danny pushed open the kitchen screen, Carolyn was sitting at the table, finishing up her work on the books.

'Making money?' Danny asked, taking a glass from the rack and filling it with water from the tap.

'You bet. We keep our overheads conservative. That's mostly the trouble with businesses today. They've been overextended.'

'I agree,' Danny said, standing with her back to the sink, sipping her water. 'You've got a nice, neat operation here.'

'Haven't we just?' Carolyn closed the

ledger. 'How did you get on with Andrew?'

'Fine. I didn't take out the notebook — he didn't want me to. Yet he was forthcoming and told me lots of things.'

'That's good. You know what we'll do? We'll invite him to the barbecue on Saturday evening.'

'We haven't been to the dance yet,' Danny said.

Carolyn grinned. 'Then by Saturday things should be warmed up.'

3

Supper, another family affair, was as enjoyable as the night before. Doug was present to cook the fish the boys had caught the day before. While he made fillets of the fish and fried them in a buttered pan, Danny and Carolyn sliced juicy tomatoes from their garden and fresh lemons to squeeze over the fish, and scrubbed and pricked potatoes for microwave baking. The meal was delicious. Danny complimented the chef and the fishermen.

As they sat on the patio after a swim, Danny felt that she was witnessing a good marriage between her cousin and his wife. They seemed to share cooking, discipline of the children, and life in general. Like her parents. It was the type of marriage she wanted for herself one day — if she ever met the right man.

In the morning Danny helped Carolyn with the laundry, taking the opportunity to rinse out some of her own garments. Instead of using the dryer, Carolyn hung most of the washing out on the line. Danny, who didn't have space enough for a clothesline at home, popped outside every once in a while, just to smell the fresh laundry as it dried quickly in the hot sun.

With time to spare, she played ball with Panda and Thunder until they grew tired and slunk away in the shade to doze beneath the trees. Then she went for a swim in the pool to cool off. It was wonderful to have relaxation time.

When she was out and dressed again, Carolyn handed her a package. 'Drop over and see how Andrew is doing with your car and give him this fish.'

'Can I walk from here?'

'Sure you can. It's a much shorter walk than drive. You see that path through the trees out back? Follow it and you'll come to Andrew's house. No hassle.'

'He might not appreciate my dropping over with no warning,' Danny said.

'You're taking him the fish. Don't show him your journalist persona. Go as yourself. Besides, if you didn't do it, I'd have to.'

'All right,' Danny said. Carolyn had enough to do without having to rush over to Andrew's with a package of fish.

'Go on,' Carolyn urged. 'The fish will go bad.'

Danny decided she would never hear the end of it from Carolyn if she didn't go. Besides, it was a pleasant walk along a well-trod grassy path between shady trees. She imagined that Andrew and the Cannons used this shortcut back and forth from their place to Andrew's all the time.

When she reached Andrew's, Sadie barked and Andrew came to the porch.

'Hi,' he said. 'Come on in. I'm baking bread.'

She was relieved he didn't seem

upset over her visit. 'You bake your own bread?'

'Mother and Dad always did, and I think the taste stuck because I don't like store-bought.'

They walked into the kitchen together. Danny handed him the fish. 'From Carolyn — caught by the boys. It's delicious.'

'Thank you. I'll put it in the fridge. Do you want a pop?'

'I'd love one, thanks. I walked over via the shady path, but it's still hot. It must be heading for ninety.'

'Close to that, I believe. It's crazy to be baking bread today, but I ran out.'

When Danny had a glass of pop to drink, she sat on one of the heavy kitchen chairs to watch Andrew soften yeast with water and sugar. He put the yeast mixture aside while he scalded milk in a pan and added fat, sugar, and salt. He put that mixture aside as well.

'What now?' she asked.

'Leave the yeast ten minutes and cool the other mixture. Then mix it with flour, and we have dough.'

Danny smiled. 'I thought making bread was more complex.'

'This is a no-fail family recipe. Grandmother's.'

'Has it ever failed you?'

'Sometimes.'

Danny didn't laugh. There was something very appealing about a strong man who made his own bread.

Andrew grabbed a pop for himself, and they went to the porch, where it was cool. Sadie lapped at her bowl of water.

'She wilts in this weather,' Andrew said as they sat down on the porch steps. 'While the bread's rising, we'll take her out to the lake for a swim. Did you want to see your car?'

'Is there much to see?'

'An engine taken apart.'

'Then why bother?'

'True. Although I can fiddle with car engines for hours.'

'You know what they're all about,' Danny said, putting down her empty glass beside her. 'You didn't mind my popping over today, did you?'

'No. Carolyn phoned to say you were on your way, actually.'

'Oh, she did?' Danny laughed. 'That lady is incorrigible.'

'She means well. But you probably wish you could be going.'

'Not immensely. I'm enjoying it here. It's nice getting to know Doug. He's a bit like my brother.'

'Your dead brother.'

She nodded.

'That's really too bad. So young.'

They sat in silence for a second. Then Andrew stood up. 'Let's go put the dough in pans.'

They washed their hands at the sink with a piece of pink soap and used a striped towel to dry off. Then Danny greased the pans while Andrew kneaded the dough. The raw, yeasty aroma filled the kitchen.

When he'd kneaded to his satisfaction, Andrew placed the dough in the pans and covered them with muslin cloths, then said, 'Hopefully, they'll rise. It's always a gamble if they will or not. We'll take Sadie for her swim now.'

They left the house by the back door. Andrew whistled to Sadie, who, as if knowing a swim was in store, burst with renewed energy.

Out back there was a garden with crisp lettuce, carrots, beets, and potatoes in neat rows. The vegetables were planted alongside marigolds, which Danny knew helped to ward off pests. Andrew really was into organic. She liked that.

They walked around the garden into a cool, earthy grove of trees and along a dirt path.

'The mosquitoes can be bad,' Andrew warned as Sadie bounded ahead, refreshed by the shade that dropped the temperature.

'I know,' Danny said. 'I just batted one off my arm. No worry. It's lovely and cool.'

'Are the summers as hot in Buffalo?'

'Yes, although more humid because

of the Great Lakes.'

'How about the winters?'

'Changeable. Sometimes we have a lot of snow, also because of the lakes. Lake-effect snow, they call it. Then sometimes the winters are mild. There's a saying in Buffalo — if you don't like the weather, wait a minute.'

Andrew chuckled. 'It's pretty certain here. Cold in winter, pretty nice in summer.'

Because Andrew had called his lake a swimming hole, Danny was surprised by its size. The water glistened beneath the hot sun; the far shore was edged by silver-barked poplars and slim pines. On their side there was a sandy beach nestled between outcrops of rocks and trees.

A yellow canoe was turned over on the wooden dock. Danny walked onto the dock beside Andrew, feeling the wood give slightly beneath her feet. A slight breeze off the lake ruffled her hair.

Sadie snooped around the beach,

then plunged into the water. Andrew stood, one booted foot raised on the end of the canoe. 'What do you think?'

'That you're lucky to have all this property, the freedom of your own land.'

'Where do you live?'

'I have a sizable townhouse to myself. One bedroom to sleep in, one for my office. My yard is a little square piece of land — a bit of grass and a few flowers. And it's close to a main road, an intersection. Some summer nights all I hear is screeching tires, not crickets. I was listening to the crickets last night at Carolyn's, and it was wonderful.'

'Ever thought of moving anywhere like this?'

'I'd love a country estate.'

'I suppose. Having lived here all my life, I've often been tempted to try city life. I did when I was in college and liked it a lot. It was exciting, but I missed the freedom. You're right about that.' He glanced at her. 'It's isolated here, though. The nearest cities,

Winnipeg, Duluth, and Minneapolis, are all a good drive.'

'Pinedale seemed to have most things anyone would want.'

'Not anyone,' he said with a deep sigh.

Danny wondered if he was thinking about the woman who went home to Boston. Did she find it isolated here? Was that why she'd left him?

Sadie ambled on the deck, soaking wet. She shook. Andrew and Danny were spattered and split apart, laughing.

'Thanks so much, Sadie,' Andrew said. '*Sit*.' Sadie plopped down on the deck. 'Good girl.' He looked at Danny. 'Do you want a canoe ride? I like paddling out on the lake. Sometimes at night I take the canoe out and sit and watch the stars. When there's a full moon in midsummer, it's like the light of day, and the water looks like oil. In daylight the water shines.'

'You've sold a canoe ride,' Danny said.

Andrew turned over the canoe.

Beneath it were two orange life jackets and two paddles. He handed Danny one of the life preservers. 'Put it on this way.'

Danny tugged the jacket over her head, adjusted it around her body, and tied the tapes.

Then Andrew slipped the canoe down a ramp into the water and climbed in without rocking it. Sadie followed him. Danny walked down the ramp. Andrew held the boat secure with a paddle jammed against the dock while she settled on the slim bench.

Andrew handed her the other paddle. 'You have to help.'

'I've canoed only once, in an amusement park with my father.'

'Do what I do. Sadie balances us.'

They dipped the paddles in and out of the water, navigating the canoe across the shimmery, calm surface.

'We'll keep close to the edge,' Andrew promised.

They paddled along the shore. About the time when Danny felt her shoulders and arms buckling from the action of paddling, Andrew said, 'Stop paddling for a moment.'

She copied him, holding the paddle horizontal. The canoe floated.

This was what Danny liked about Andrew — his ability to catch a moment. This moment was silent and brilliant until a fish jumped the surface.

Sadie barked; the canoe rocked perilously.

Andrew said to Danny, 'Paddle. Keep the boat upright.'

Danny had to think quickly which side to paddle.

Sadie barked again and leaped. Andrew moved stealthily forward. The canoe rocked as if it had been hit by a huge wave.

Andrew grabbed Sadie's collar and dragged her back from the edge of the canoe. 'Sit,' he commanded.

Sadie sat, looking sheepish.

'You nearly dumped us, you stupid dog,' Andrew said, picking up his paddle and helping to steer once more.

He glanced at Danny. 'Are you okay?'

'Fine.'

Peril avoided, they both began laughing.

'Oh, Sadie,' Danny said. 'Is it deep?' she asked Andrew.

'Deep enough so we'd have to swim. The only place you can stand up is a few feet from my beach; then it drops.'

'I think I could swim it with the life jacket,' Danny said. 'It's cold, though, isn't it?'

'It's not too bad this time of year. We'd have made it fine, but any other time of the year, even with life jackets, hypothermia can set in, and it's really uncomfortable in clothes.'

'Speaking from experience?' Danny asked.

'Am I ever!' Andrew laughed. 'And from experience I would say that today we've had enough.'

He steered the canoe back to the dock, let Sadie and Danny disembark, then tugged the canoe up the ramp and turned it upside down once more, paddles and jackets underneath.

'Thank you,' Danny said. 'That was fun.'

'No thanks to Sadie here.' Andrew picked up a stick and threw it for the dog so she'd run in the direction of the path.

They returned to the house, where the bread was in the midst of rising. Danny didn't stick around any longer. She felt she'd stayed her welcome. She walked back to Carolyn and Doug's and found the kids in the pool. Carolyn, wearing her swimsuit, was on a lounger, reading a magazine.

'This is my happy hour,' Carolyn said. 'Have a swim if you want. Make the most of your time off. Did you see Andrew and give him the fish?'

'Yes. We made bread — or Andrew made bread and I watched. Then we walked to the lake so Sadie could swim. We went for a canoe ride, and I almost did have a swim when Sadie jumped at a fish.'

Carolyn smiled. 'How do you feel about him?'

Danny sat down in a cushioned patio chair. 'Who?'

'Andrew, of course.'

'He's very nice. However, I can't allow myself to feel anything more than friendship. I'll be leaving next week.'

'You can always come and live with him here.'

'You're talking about marriage, aren't you?'

'Andrew wouldn't go for anything except marriage, believe me. He's one of the last of the old-fashioned men. Besides, it can get pretty gossipy around here, and Andrew's respected. It's not worth the hassle to try to be too modern.'

Danny's fingers ran along the arm of the chair. 'The woman who went back to Boston, Carolyn. Why did she return?'

'Because she didn't love Andrew enough to give anything up.'

'Maybe she had family and her job back there.'

'Some family, I believe, but she worked here. She didn't like being so far away from city life.'

'Did Andrew tell you this?'

Carolyn laid aside her magazine on a small plastic table. 'In a roundabout way he told Doug.'

'I thought I sensed an adversary when he found out I was from the East. He didn't like my saying stuff about Middle America.'

'It's probably because of Lise. But you're nothing like her. You're much more sensitive. She wasn't right for him.'

'Neither am I. My work takes a great deal of my time.'

'So does Andrew's. And he has someone who comes in once a week to do the house. You would have plenty of time for your own endeavors.'

Danny sighed. 'You make it sound as if we've already fallen in love and we have to make a decision about what to do.'

'Haven't you?'

'No. I'm only getting to know him. And I'm not going to fall in love with him. I won't be around. I'm not going to hurt him — although I doubt if he'd fall in love with me.'

'He likes you.'

'He's friendly, but he's been forced to be with me, Carolyn. And you're not helping any.'

Carolyn grinned. 'Am I very obvious?'

'Very obvious.'

'Andrew's not mad?'

'No. He's not mad. At least not outwardly.'

'After you've left, he'll give me a word or two, I bet. Maybe I'll lay off for a while and let nature take its course.'

That'll be the day, Danny thought, hiding a smile. But somehow, she didn't blame Carolyn. If circumstances were different, she could almost picture a future for her and Andrew. If only things were different . . .

As the kids weren't going to be home for supper, Doug told Carolyn and

Danny that if they wore their best jeans, he'd take them for burgers. It took no coaxing to get Carolyn to leave the house for a while, and they all piled into Doug's truck, Danny on the seat in the rear passenger cab.

As they drove along the gravel road, with windows wound down, letting in a coarse, hot breeze, Carolyn said, 'Go honk Andrew and see if he wants to join us.'

Doug turned into Andrew's driveway. He stopped the truck and rammed his fist on the horn.

Sadie barked. Andrew came out, wearing no shoes or shirt with his jeans. He quickly shoved his feet into a pair of battered sneakers on the porch and grabbed a shirt that was drying on the line. He buttoned it as he came over to Doug's truck.

'What's happening?' he asked, leaning in the window. He saw Danny and smiled.

'We're going for junk food. Wanna come?' Carolyn asked.

'I was going to have an organically grown salad with your kid's fish.'

'If you're really into self-flagellation, you can have one of those new light burgers,' Doug said. 'And the fish can wait.'

Andrew laughed. 'Okay. Give me a sec to close down.'

He went into the house and returned in his boots and his clean white shirt, the sleeves rolled up. He tucked his lean body in beside Danny.

'It's nice having you here, Danny,' Carolyn said. 'We haven't done neat stuff like this for ages. We get staid in our old age.'

'Speak for your own old age,' Andrew countered, resting his arms on the back of Carolyn's seat. 'Danny and I are still beneath the thirty mark.'

'You've only got another year or so, Andrew,' Carolyn reminded him. 'You should be married before you're thirty. If you don't have kids young enough, you'll be a granddad to your own offspring.'

'I've got your kids.'

'Do you want them?' Doug asked. 'You can have 'em. We're always sending them over to friends' houses. The darnedest part is, they always return.'

Danny laughed. 'You guys have a great family.'

'I suppose we're lucky,' Carolyn said.

'Very lucky,' Andrew agreed, and Danny thought she heard a wistfulness in his tone.

Andrew, Carolyn, and Doug were known in the fast-food burger joint. The waitresses were friendly, and so were the patrons of the restaurant, especially a woman with bright auburn hair who came over to Andrew and said, 'We haven't seen you at the dances lately.'

'I haven't been, that's why,' he said.

'Are you coming this Friday?'

'Yes. I am. With Danny here.'

Carolyn said, 'Danny is Doug's cousin from Buffalo, New York. Danny, this is Rosemary Smith.'

'Hi, Rosemary,' Danny greeted her.

'Hi, Danny. Pleased to meet you. You'll enjoy the dance.' Rosemary turned back to Andrew. 'So we'll see you at the dance tomorrow night. 'Bye.'

'Trouble brewing,' Doug said.

'She's been after Andrew for years,' Carolyn told him. 'Andrew can deal with her.'

Danny glanced at Andrew. 'Am I cramping your style? Because if I am, you don't have to be my date.'

'I want you to be my date,' he said.

'Good.' She heard a crack in her voice. It would be easy to fall in love with Andrew. Far too easy.

On the way home in the truck, everyone was tired after a long, hot day, and silent. The now cooler breeze played with Danny's hair, and she was intensely aware of Andrew by her side.

'Want to come back for a while?' Carolyn asked Andrew.

'No, it's okay. I have to give Sadie a

run to the lake. She hasn't been fed yet.'

Probably he's had enough of being pushed on me, Danny thought as Doug drove into Andrew's place. Andrew got out of the truck. Without him beside her, she felt as if part of her had been chopped off.

'We'll come by for the dance tomorrow evening,' Carolyn reminded him.

'See you all then,' he said.

Before the truck turned behind the trees, Danny looked back and saw him walking up the porch steps.

'I wish I didn't have to go to the dance with him,' Danny said. 'I feel like I'm a real imposition on him. It's enough that he towed my car to his house and is fixing it.'

Carolyn eyed her over the back of the seat. 'You're not thinking of Rosemary, I hope.'

'Of course I'm thinking of Rosemary. He obviously has girlfriends here.'

'No, he doesn't. That's the point. He

rarely dates. This is a great opportunity to get him out and about. Even if nothing happens between you two, at least he'll get the message that there's a world of fun out there.'

'You can't organize people's lives, Carolyn,' Danny said.

'Oh, yes, she can,' Doug insisted. 'And don't worry about Andrew, Danny. Believe me, if he truly didn't want to take you to the dance, then he wouldn't.'

Danny wasn't so sure about that. Andrew couldn't very well turn them all down. That not only would be embarrassing to Danny, but Carolyn and Doug as well.

Danny worried all night and spent Friday feeling anxious about the evening to come. She wanted to slip away, either to the telephone or along the path that led to Andrew's house, but she didn't get a chance. Carolyn asked her to watch the boys in the pool in the morning while she went out on business. In the afternoon it was hot,

4

Danny had calmed down a bit by the time she slipped her new rose-pink cotton sundress over her head on Friday evening. She zipped it and enjoyed the way the soft cotton fell around her slim body. Rarely did she wear a dress, as most of the time she was home working on her computer in sweats or shorts. To do so now felt feminine, almost glamorous. Maybe Carolyn was right; people did need a change once in a while, a chance to be a different type of person for an evening.

Around her neck she placed a short silver chain with a heart locket containing photos of her brother. Then she stuffed a few things, including a tiny notebook, into a small white leather purse and gazed at herself in the mirror. She looked nice. A country girl going to a country dance? Or a city woman, masquerading as a country girl? Did Andrew think that? Was this interlude comparable to the time she went to Jamaica and for those two weeks really got into the tropical life? She wore straw hats, sandals, swimsuits, shorts, and flowing cotton dresses and hated returning to winter to dress up in heavy coats and boots once more. Then after a time she acclimatized, and Jamaica became a dream. Would Drake Farm become a similar dream?

Doug took the kids to a neighbor's for the night, returned to the house, and dressed in a dark suit; then, in the minivan, they went to call on Andrew. He moved in beside Danny on the rear seat, wearing a charcoal sports jacket, lighter slacks, and a white shirt and blue tie. He smelled nice and fresh.

'You look wonderful,' he told Danny. 'Pink suits you. Is that the new dress?'

Surprised by his interest, she said, 'Yes. Local fare.'

'Pretty.' Andrew leaned forward and tapped Carolyn's shoulder. 'You look fancy too, Caro.'

Carolyn turned around to look at them. 'Thanks, Andy. You're spiffy yourself. And Doug's out of the Stetson and boots for one night. Can you believe it?'

'I feel naked,' Doug said as they sped along the highway, the warm evening air slipping in his open window. He glanced at his wife and smiled tenderly.

Danny felt her heart contract. Wouldn't it be nice, she thought, to find a comradeship like the one shared by her cousin and his wife? Equal partners in life together. Rarely did she think of marriage the way she'd been thinking of it since she'd been here the past few days. Whether it was Andrew's presence or Doug and Carolyn's example, she wasn't particularly keen to analyze.

They passed the fast-food restaurant they had gone to last night, and Doug slowed the van as they entered town. 'That's our high school,' he told Danny. 'I met Carolyn at Pinedale High.'

'Years before Andrew went, of course,' Carolyn said.

'Some of my teachers were the same,' Andrew remarked.

'And they seemed old when we went,' Doug said. 'They must have been doddering by the time they reached you, Andy.'

Andrew chuckled. 'Ancient.'

'Teachers aren't ancient anymore,' Carolyn said. 'When I go to PTA, all the teachers are younger than I. Pretty and bright too.' She patted her husband's arm. 'I'm pleased they weren't like that in our time. Doug would have had too many distractions to notice me.'

Andrew smiled across at Danny as if to say, *They're always this way. Loving, teasing, a real couple.* Did he want a marriage like that? Had he hoped for a marriage like that with Lise? Had all his dreams fallen apart?

They parked the van and walked up the street as two couples — Doug and Carolyn in front, Andrew and Danny trailing. Danny was getting used to being paired with Andrew now — too used to it.

The hall was a building that appeared to have been a movie theater once, because the marquee was still up.

'This is where I took my dates,' Doug said. 'Sure was fun.'

'The dates or the movies?' Carolyn asked.

'The movies, of course, dear,' Doug said and grinned over at Danny.

Doug paid the admission for them all. Danny wished he wouldn't, but he insisted. The Cannons' hospitality so far had been exemplary. She made a resolution to take them all out to some fancy restaurant on the evening before she left for home.

If there was once a movie theater inside the building, the only sign of its presence was the podium and the sweep of heavy curtains at each end. On the podium a band warmed up. A bar was set up at one side of the hall.

'We'll bag a table,' Carolyn said,

ushering them all ahead of her as if she were herding sheep. 'Look, there's Bill and Tammy. We'll sit with them.'

Danny was introduced to the middle-aged couple, who invited them to join their table.

'Danny's here from Buffalo, New York,' Carolyn explained. 'She's a writer and is researching an article about farms. So if she asks you questions, answer them nicely.'

'Buffalo, New York,' Tammy said. 'That's a ways away.'

'An article,' Bill added. 'Interesting.'

'Now,' Doug said, standing, 'I'll buy the first round of drinks. Orders, please.'

By the time Doug returned with the drinks, the band had begun to play and a singer was imitating Elvis with a breathy, slightly out-of-tune version of 'Love Me Tender.' Danny hid her chuckle, although not enough, it seemed.

Andrew, who was sitting beside her, said, 'I noticed that. I suppose this dance isn't sophisticated enough for you.'

'That's not true. I think it's wonderful and — ' She almost added *charming*, but remembered her candy-coated foot. 'I'm having a great time. And don't be so touchy. I'm not putting you down. It's only that my mom was such an Elvis fan, I grew up on his records and know them backward and forward, and when something's out of tune, it sounds . . . out of tune.'

'It is out of tune, I'll admit,' Andrew agreed with a smile. 'Does that mean you won't want to dance?'

'I'd love to dance.'

'Then let's go.'

They stood up, and Carolyn said, 'Oh, they're going to dance. Wonderful! Have fun, kids.'

'Kids,' Andrew repeated, putting his arms around Danny on the dance floor. 'She sounds like Mother Earth.'

Danny laughed, avoiding how she felt in Andrew's embrace. She didn't say, as she almost did, that Carolyn wanted

99

him married so there'd be another woman around. She didn't want to get into all that with him tonight — or any night, for that matter. She had to remind herself that this evening was as temporary as her stay here.

'You're not really going to mix this evening with business, are you?' Andrew asked as they danced.

'What do you mean?'

'Carolyn said you were going to ask questions. Farmers come here to relax, to forget their everyday problems, not to be reminded of them.'

'Just because Carolyn says something doesn't mean I'm going to do it,' Danny pointed out.

'I hope not.'

'Andrew, you're going to have to get over this.'

'Over what?'

'Over what you think I am, compared to what I really am.'

At that moment the lights dimmed. Wolf whistles, hoots, and hollers were shouted from the tables.

'Hold her tight,' the band leader said and led his group into a melodic pop song.

Danny felt Andrew's arms tighten around her. Her breath quickened.

Slow dancing . . . Andrew's golden hair brushing her cheek . . . her hair spilling over his shoulder. It would be so easy, Danny thought, to fall in love.

Yet she couldn't do any such thing. When her car was fixed, she was going home to Buffalo, and that was that. She certainly didn't want to give in to impulses that might in turn hurt Andrew. He'd been hurt once. He was too nice. Too lonely. Much too lonely and vulnerable for a fling that didn't go anywhere.

Even though she was on the brink of something that bordered on happiness, Danny was pleased when the slow set ended and they walked back to their table.

The lights remained lowered, with a pink spotlight hovering over the dance floor.

'Doug says he can't dance without his boots on,' Carolyn said.

'I'll dance with you,' Andrew offered. 'Come on.'

Left alone with Doug, Danny smiled. 'This is fun.'

'Carolyn loves it. She's always loved dances. I don't know why she married a klutz like me.'

'Because she loves you.'

'That's the truth, Danny. I couldn't live without her, you know.'

Danny touched his big, rough hand. 'That's good to hear. Most of the couples I know are saying the opposite.'

'You have to admit it to yourself and make yourself a little vulnerable,' Doug said.

'I'll keep that in mind for when I meet the man of my dreams.' As she spoke, Danny turned to glance at Andrew, who was laughing with Carolyn as they danced fast apart.

'Could Andrew be that?' Doug asked.

She turned her attention back to her cousin. 'Doug, I'm not here looking for a boyfriend. I have a career back in Buffalo.'

'I know. But we were discussing it last night, and Carolyn and I both agree that Andrew needs a wife.'

'Not me, though, Doug.'

'Don't you like him?'

'Of course I like him, but I'm not ready to get married.'

'You're over twenty-six, aren't you? Carolyn was twenty when we got married. I was only twenty-two.'

'That's you guys. It's different for everyone.'

'I know, but . . . Carolyn would like another woman around.'

'Andrew will meet someone. One day.'

'We hope so.'

More friends stopped by their table, other farmers. Carolyn introduced Danny to all of them and told each one that Danny was from New York, researching an article. Danny listened to their colorful stories, fervently wishing she had her tape recorder with her, but reminding herself what Andrew had told her. The farmers were here to relax, to forget everyday problems. In a backhanded way she'd promised him she wouldn't ask questions or take notes.

Then why were they talking farm talk? More than likely it was the same as any members of an occupation when they got together — a chance to exchange stories, ideas, theories; a place to be accepted. There were a number of fellow writers she kept in contact with. They understood one another's woes without question. Farmers were similar in a way. They needed to carve a living from a blank piece of land the way writers carved stories from blank sheets of paper. And it was comforting to know someone else suffered the same problems or had an answer to a problem.

Nonetheless, some of the information was too good to let slip, so in a moment when Andrew wasn't at the table, Danny grabbed her purse, slipped into the powder room, and wrote some notes quickly in her small notepad.

Feeling she'd heard some excellent tidbits to fill out her article, she left the powder room with a certain amount of exuberance and almost bumped into Andrew, who was standing in the hallway near the open door, getting a breath of fresh air.

'I wondered where you'd gone,' he said.

She wasn't going to tell him she'd written some notes. So she said, 'I needed to powder my nose.'

'You don't look as if you wear much makeup.'

'I don't, silly.' She gave him a look.

His cheekbones flushed, and she thought that was sweet. 'I get you,' he said. 'Are you enjoying yourself?'

'I'm having a great time.'

'Even with the tainted Elvis?'

Danny smiled. 'You get used to him after a while. He did a good version of 'Jailhouse Rock.' 'Love Me Tender' is a difficult song to sing.'

'True.' He loosened his tie. 'Do you want to dance again?'

She nodded. 'Love to.'

They returned to the table. Andrew discarded his jacket, and Danny left her purse. After the fast set Andrew went to get them both cold drinks. Danny sat alone at the table waiting for him, something inside her aching for what wasn't going to be.

After her drink Danny danced with her cousin. When Doug led her back to the table, Carolyn, Bill, and Tammy were there. Andrew was absent.

'He got nabbed by Rosemary Smith,' Carolyn said. 'Rosemary has had a crush on him since high school. They dated a few times, though Andrew never showed much interest. He's too polite to turn her down.'

'She asked him to dance?' Danny asked.

'Yes. That's the way it is these days.'

Danny's gaze searched the dancing couples for Rosemary and Andrew. Much to Danny's relief the couple talked as they danced. Now she was becoming possessive, she thought. She should be pleased Andrew had a hometown woman interested in him.

Still, the longer Andrew danced with Rosemary, the more agitated Danny became inside. However, she didn't show her agitation. She sat calmly, sipping her drink, and when he returned, she smiled serenely.

'Let's dance again,' he said, his tone sounding as if he'd missed her.

She went into his arms on the dance floor. This time instead of holding her waist and hand, dancing formally, he cupped his hands at the small of her back, so she had to wind her arms around his neck. Then it seemed natural to move slightly closer. She was sure she felt his lips brush her hair.

When they leaned apart after the set and gazed at each other, Danny wanted to rush away from Andrew, from all the feelings gathered inside her. She was ready to tell Andrew she didn't want to dance any longer, when the band leader said, 'Now grab your honey for the last set and the *last* dance. Everyone up now. I don't want to see a soul sitting on the edge looking like a wallflower. Or maybe I should say wallperson.'

'I guess we're here for the duration,' Andrew said.

'I guess.' Danny's breathing wasn't even; her legs were unsteady. His hands felt warm on her spine. Her fingers fought with themselves not to stroke his golden hair. She held herself tense. An anxiety attack was in the making.

The music for the final set began. The singer seemed to improve as the evening wore on, when he didn't try to imitate Elvis. Danny saw Carolyn and Doug dancing dreamily together. Good old Doug. He roused himself for the last dance. He wouldn't let Carolyn down on that one, because he loved her. And it was true; he didn't dance that well. Unlike Andrew, who seemed to have an inbred sense of what step to put to what note.

Except Danny was so shaky that her

sandaled feet kept bumping his shoes. He likely thought she was a real dope. Wasn't she supposed to be the sophisticated one? The city girl?

'The *last* dance,' the bandleader said. 'Hold her tight.'

The strains of the song began. The singer crooned. Nothing like a love song and a good-looking man in your arms to mess up your senses, Danny thought. But real life wasn't this. Real life was outside this hall: Andrew on his farm with his view of trees and sunflower fields, Danny in her townhouse with her view of other brick walls.

'Danny,' Andrew said softly, leaning down to her, 'it's over.'

The entire dance was over. The band was clearing away its gear. They'd done their job; on to their next gig. People were stacking chairs and tables. Some were heading for the door.

'Farmers are early risers,' Andrew said as they walked over to Carolyn and Doug. 'Ready to leave?' he asked them.

'No. But who has a choice?' Carolyn said. 'I just get this guy in a romantic mood, and it ends. Wouldn't you know it!'

'I'm still in a romantic mood,' Doug told her, taking her hand. 'Come on. We'll go grab something to eat.'

Outside, the air still held the heat of the day. Haze rose from the sidewalks.

Andrew gently touched Danny's waist to steer her beside him on the sidewalk.

Carolyn was still in a dancing mood, holding on to Doug's arm. 'I could have danced all night,' she sang.

Andrew chuckled. 'Do we know them?'

'I'm related to them.'

'Pretend you aren't.'

Danny grinned.

They reached the van, and Doug unlocked the doors. Danny sat in the back beside Andrew. Close. He stretched his arm behind her on the seat, not touching, but almost. She wanted him to touch, but she didn't.

Talk about confusion.

Doug drove to the restaurant beside the Pinedale Motor Lodge. Most of the customers straggling in had been at the dance.

'Hi, Doug.'

'Hi, Carolyn.'

'Hi, Andy.'

A stare or two for Danny. *Who is she? With Andrew?*

'Have a good time?' a couple asked.

'We're going to have to lobby for dances every week instead of once a month,' Carolyn said.

'I wish they were every week,' the gray-haired waitress said as she poured coffee all around and took orders for the fries they would share. 'Business would boom.'

'Business always booms here, Gracie,' Doug said.

'It's slowed down since they put up another fast-food place. We have to wait until folks realize that we do good down-home cooking.'

'Folks realize that. You know it.

You've had the monopoly for years.'

'That we have,' Gracie said and toddled off to put in their order.

'Is she the owner?' Danny asked.

Andrew, sitting in the booth beside her, said, 'Yes. She'll go down with the ship.'

'She's rolling in cash,' Doug countered. 'Don't let her moaning get to you. For years this was the only decent restaurant in the vicinity.'

'I like it,' Danny said.

'We wouldn't come here if we didn't,' Carolyn said. 'It's never changed. That's its charm.'

When their order arrived, Danny found her arm brushed Andrew's each time she reached for a fry. The sensations were equivalent to rubbing two stones together. Her insides felt like a fire about to ignite.

Even during the drive home she was still very tense and stared out the window at the warm lights in the windows of farmhouses. Forms of trees and barns loomed in a sky that appeared luminous, as if it never got truly dark in these parts during the summer.

When Andrew's palm brushed hers on the seat between them, she glanced down and then into his eyes. But he didn't hold her hand.

Doug stopped the van outside Andrew's house.

'Good night,' Andrew said as he slipped across the seat to leave. 'It was a good time.'

'It was,' Carolyn said. 'Enjoy yourself, Danny?'

'I sure did. I took lots of notes from the farmers.'

Andrew was out of the van now, leaning in. His jaw appeared taut.

'I didn't see you taking notes,' he said.

'I remember stuff,' Danny told him. What a *faux pas*! Her candy-coated foot again. *Oh, Len, you were so right!*

'That's all you're using us for, isn't it? Research. We're like a bunch of insects under a microscope to you.'

'No.' Danny said, moving along the seat so she was closer to him. 'That's not true.'

He glanced at Carolyn and Doug. 'Thanks for the lift and the nice evening. See you all tomorrow night at the barbecue.'

He yanked the door shut on the van, and Danny watched from the window as he strode into the house. She heard Sadie bark as he unlocked the front door.

If she were alone, she would go after him to try to explain. But what did you say to a man who was convinced that she thought he wasn't quite up to her class of people? And why bother saying anything when in a few days she would be gone from here?

Doug drove on. 'You said the wrong thing, Danny.'

'I'm sorry. But I *am* here to work, and it was such an opportunity tonight. I didn't mean to tell him I wrote down some notes. I did it secretly in the ladies' room. Besides, he said farmers were at the dance to relax, and all they talked about was farming. Maybe with a little time off for baseball scores.'

'That's so true. So forget it,' Carolyn said. 'Andrew will get over his snit. You'll see tomorrow night.'

'Maybe I shouldn't socialize with him anymore,' Danny said.

'Heavens, why not? You're our guest, and Andrew needs to come out of his shell and live a little.'

Danny kept silent after that. She didn't want to hurt Andrew, and yet she was the one person who seemed to be able to — with her big mouth.

In her bedroom she took off the dress, hung it in the closet, and, with an oversized T-shirt on, washed her face, brushed her teeth and her hair, and went to bed.

She couldn't sleep. She tossed one way, then the other. She felt really bad about upsetting Andrew after the dance and wanted to apologize.

As soon as it was light, she got up, dressed, and went downstairs. No one was around. There was coffee and a note propped against the coffee maker. *All gone out. Saturday morning in town. Enjoy the peace. C & D.* She smiled, put the note down on the table, and drank two cups of coffee to boost her confidence as well as make her more wide-awake. Then she set out to Andrew's house.

All along the path she rehearsed her speech to Andrew. *I'm sorry you were stuck with me last night, but we couldn't upset Carolyn and not go together. I didn't mean to upset you, either. I'm sorry.*

He wasn't there. Neither was Sadie. And Rolfe didn't want to be disturbed. He frowned and hid his face between his paws when he saw her.

Danny went to the lake, remembering the day she had walked side by side with Andrew. The yellow canoe was upturned, the way they had left it the other day. The water lapped gently on the shore. Danny sat down on the dock, slipped off her canvas shoes, and dangled her feet over the edge into the cool water.

She wondered what it would be like to live here always, to wake up every morning in the summer and walk by the lake before settling down to work for the day. With computers and fax machines, her career permitted her to live anywhere.

In the winter the snow would crunch beneath her feet and the lake would freeze. She could skate, toboggan, cross-country ski — all those things she could do in New York State but never made the time for. Because at home everything was a rushabout. Out here there seemed to be time, as expansive as the land. Or was it that she was stuck between time with her car out of service?

Whatever it was, she was feeling decidedly unsettled — with her life back home, with her life in general. And she'd thought she had it so good! Well, she did. But she still missed Len terribly. She'd never recover from his sudden tragic death; she knew that now. The entire family carried his life with them like a memory to cherish.

Danny splashed her feet. Droplets sparkled in the sunshine and spattered onto the dock. Oh, dear. It was Andrew who had caused this introspective mood. Andrew with his golden hair, his special smile, and his loneliness.

She stood up and walked barefoot up the dock before putting on her shoes. When she reached the house, Andrew still wasn't home. She thought about leaving a note but didn't feel it was quite the way she wanted to touch base with him. Besides, she would see him tonight at the barbecue.

5

When Danny returned to Carolyn and Doug's, they were all home once more, their house noisy as they enjoyed themselves in their disorganized, friendly way.

Carolyn said as she unpacked cans, 'We wondered where you were.'

Danny moved beside her to help with the grocery unpacking. 'I went for a walk.'

'Are you okay?'

'Fine. I'm not used to late nights and dances.'

'Neither are we, but it does you good to get out and kick up your heels once in a blue moon. We ran into Andrew in town. He said he really had a good time.'

'He did?'

'Of course he did. And don't you think otherwise, just because he acted like a clown last night.' Carolyn peered at Danny the way she looked at the children when she wasn't quite sure what they were up to. 'You haven't been worried about it, have you?'

'A little,' Danny admitted.

'Don't be. He doesn't mean it.'

'He must if he says it. I'm not here to be condescending to any of you.'

'I know that; Doug knows that. And Andrew will learn it as he gets to know you. But if you want to take your mind off him for a sec, you can help out as we've got quite a crowd coming for the barbecue. If you go downstairs to the basement freezer, you'll find frozen corn. Take out enough to feed nine. Keep in mind the women usually eat only one cob, but the men and kids can put away at least three or four.'

'I'll do that for you. Anything else?'

'If I think of it, I'll tell you. Doug does the barbecuing.'

'That's nice,' Danny said. 'Doug's a gem.'

'I know. That's why Andrew would be such an excellent husband. He looks after himself.'

'He bakes good bread.'

'Did you taste it?'

'No. It wasn't ready.'

'I'll phone him and tell him to bring a couple of loaves. Then you can taste his skills.'

'Poor Andrew. When I finally leave, he's going to say, 'Oh thank goodness!' '

Carolyn laughed.

Danny smiled.

'That's better. Cheer up. You looked quite down when I came in.'

'You cheer anyone up, Carolyn. Now I'll go hunt out that corn in the freezer. Do you need a salad?'

'If you feel so inclined.'

'My specialty. Tossed green salad.'

'Use the fresh lettuce from outdoors.'

'I will.'

With Danny's salad prepared in a wooden bowl and the corn simmering in a huge silver pot on the stove, she showered and put on a purple tank top, a pair of white cotton slacks with a white cord tie belt, and white sandals. She brushed her hair, then surveyed her reflection. She hoped she looked nice. For Andrew? Yes, probably.

Carolyn, dressed in a yellow jumpsuit, bustled out with cutlery and napkins. Danny helped. By the time the umbrella table was set, Kyle and Sean were ordered to wash up for dinner. Then Andrew arrived in a more relaxed fit of denims and a short-sleeved blue shirt that made his eyes seem bluer, if that were possible. He wore sneakers tonight and brought with him a small athletic bag.

'Swim gear,' he explained, dumping the bag into a corner of the patio.

'You can either go in before the meal or after it's gone down,' Doug said, wearing a chef's apron tied over shorts and shirt as he prepared the gas barbecue to cook chicken.

'As I've got stuff boiling in the kitchen, I'll wait until after,' Danny said.

'Me too,' Andrew told her. 'I brought bread. Hang on; I left it in the truck.'

Danny went into the kitchen to check the progress of the corn, and in a few moments Andrew came in, carrying two of his homemade loaves covered in plastic bags.

'They turned out well,' Danny said as he placed the loaves on the kitchen counter.

'They did. It must have been the way you greased the pans.'

They smiled at each other.

He raked his hand through his hair. 'Sorry about last night. But I didn't know you were taking notes, and when you told me, I was quite surprised.'

'I wasn't really taking notes, Andrew. I had a small notebook, and I wrote down a few bits I gleaned. I didn't intend for it to be a big deal.'

'I realized that afterward.' He shifted on his feet. 'I had a bad experience once.'

'I know. Carolyn told me.'

He leaned his shoulders against the

fridge door. 'Did she tell you everything?'

'I'm not sure if it was everything.
Only that you were hurt when a friend
of yours preferred city life to getting
married to you.' Danny faltered a little
over the last few words.

'That puts it quite simply. It's made
me off balance and defensive, especially
about people from cities, who sometimes feel they're superior to country
people. As if knowledge of what movie
is playing is more important than the
land. They wouldn't have food if
farmers didn't get up at the crack of
dawn, in rain, snow, sleet, or shine, to
work.'

Danny replaced the lid on the corn
pot. 'You're right. And I understand.
I'm on your side. I've also got no
intention of hurting you. Besides, my
engine should be fixed soon, and then
I'll be a puff of dust on your road.'

'Yeah.'

Danny walked over to stand in front
of him. 'We can still be friends. I'll keep

124

in contact with Doug and send you a copy of the article.'

'Yeah,' he said again and left the kitchen.

Danny sighed.

Doug's parents and Marcia arrived next. Everyone retreated with drinks to the patio to catch up on the news. Danny wanted to know her newfound relatives' lives from scratch.

Doug's parents were both retired teachers, his sister also a teacher. Because of this, Danny wondered how Doug got into farming. It seemed he worked on farms for pocket money when he was a kid and continued with the farm life after high school graduation. He lived in town with Carolyn when they were first married. Then when Andrew's father needed money for his farm to survive, he purchased some land and built his house.

'And the rest is history,' Doug said, brandishing a barbecue fork. 'Andrew's dad died, and Andrew took me on as his partner. A case of being in the right place at the right time.'

'And they've done so well,' Marcia said.

She was a big-boned woman with dark hair, like all the Cannons. Danny's mother was big-boned and dark-haired. Danny found it exciting to know she had an entire other family here in Minnesota.

The food was good — the barbecued chicken was spicy and tender, the corn sweet, the salad crunchy. Doug's parents and Marcia left after coffee, an action Carolyn said was typical of them. They didn't much care for socializing.

'My mother's the same,' Danny said. 'And the way I feel since I've been here, I'm wondering if I don't harbor similar traits. I haven't socialized like this for a long, long time.'

'Stick around here, and it's all fun,' Doug said.

'So you're not like your parents?' Danny asked.

'No way. Chalk and cheese.'

She laughed.

'Now that they've all gone, can we swim?' Sean asked.

'If you want,' Carolyn said.

'Let's play ball,' Kyle suggested. 'Us against you and Danny. Okay, Uncle Andy?'

Andrew smiled. 'Okay, if Danny wants to play.'

'I'll play,' she said. 'It seems a long time since I just fooled around.'

'All you think about is work, that's why,' he said.

'I have to make a living. Writing articles isn't the same as going to a regular job. I *make* my own work.'

'So you come and bug us farmers.'

'I didn't come to bug you on purpose. If my car hadn't broken down, I would have spent a couple of nights here with Doug and be gone by now. We might never have met.'

'And, on the other hand, we might have met.'

'On the other hand, yes,' she said.

Carolyn made a chopping motion

between them. 'Break it up, you two. Danny's our guest, Andrew. Treat her nice.'

After their dinner had settled, Danny changed for swimming in her room, while the others took turns in the cedar cabana. Then they dove from the heat into the refreshing pool.

They formed two teams: Kyle, Sean, and Doug against Carolyn, Danny, and Andrew. One bright beach ball batted back and forth. There was more water on the outer tiles than in the pool by the time they finished splashing and screaming. Danny hadn't had such a good time for years. Maybe not since before Len died.

Kyle, Sean, and Doug won six games out of ten.

'We're the winners,' Sean said, toweling down. 'We get gold medals. You guys don't rate.'

'We get silver,' Andrew insisted.

'You lost. You don't get anything.'

'Seconds get silver.'

'Only if they play other teams,' Kyle

said. 'Don't be stupid, Andrew.'

'Don't call Andrew stupid,' his father berated.

'All I do is call him stupid back,' Andrew said.

'Hey, Uncle Andy,' Kyle said, 'while Danny's here, can we go fishing on Sunflower Lake?'

'It depends on your parents, Kyle.'

'Dad won't let us fish the lake alone; it's too deep. And we promised we'd take you fishing. Didn't we, Danny?'

'You mentioned fishing,' she said, 'yes.' She wasn't sure about the promise bit.

'Is it something you want to do?' Andrew asked her. 'I've got time tomorrow morning if you want. Bright and early.'

Kyle rushed in. 'We'll be there with Danny. We'll give her a rod and bait. She can help us dig for worms.'

'Oh, great. Just what Danny's always wanted to do,' Carolyn said. 'You don't have to do this if you don't want, Danny.'

'It sounds like fun. I used to fish with Len, my brother.'

'Yeah?' Andrew said.

'Yeah, I did.' She smiled to loosen the atmosphere.

'You never mentioned you had a brother,' Carolyn said. 'Just two sisters.'

'Danny's brother died a few years back,' Andrew inserted. 'The Trans Am was his car.'

'I remember,' Doug said. 'Industrial accident or something?'

Danny nodded.

'Oh, dear,' Carolyn said. 'Well, we shouldn't be talking about it, should we? We'll upset her. So is it fishing, guys, or what?'

'Fishing,' they chorused. 'Up and at 'em in the morning, Danny.'

'Knock on my door if I'm not up,' she told them.

Doug stood up from his chair. 'Now,' he announced, 'I think it's about time you boys went up to bed. You need your fishing sleep.'

'We don't have to bathe tonight?'

'No. You're fine,' their mother said. 'Go on. Scoot.'

Danny went up to her room to change back into her clothes. Andrew and the others were also dressed when she reappeared.

Andrew picked up his bag. 'I'll see you tomorrow morning, Danny.'

'Early, but I'm not sure about the bright,' she said.

He grinned and she picked up his step to walk with him around the house to his truck. They walked leisurely, as if they did it all the time together.

''Night,' he said when he was in the truck ready to go.

''Night.'

She stepped back, and he drove off. Then she went to bed.

It didn't seem as if she had any sleep. Before she knew it, the boys rapped at her door, screaming, 'Danny! Get up!'

Dressed in jeans, a T-shirt, and a Minnesota Twins cap given to her by the boys to cover her head, Danny was soon on her way to meet Andrew for fishing, her eyes barely open as she tramped dew-laden grass and carried a rod-and-tackle box. Toad scrambled ahead, poking in holes, hoping for a rabbit.

When they reached Andrew's house, Sadie and Toad barked at each other, and the boys ran in through the back door. Andrew was in the kitchen, filling a thermos with coffee. He'd made sandwiches.

'Boys get hungry,' he said 'And you probably didn't have time for anything.'

'I drank some juice, that's all,' she admitted. 'This is really early, isn't it?'

'Fishing is early,' Andrew said.

'Did you do this a lot when you were a boy?'

'Sure did. My dad and I. We still did it until . . . until he got sick. Okay now. Kyle, you carry the picnic. Sean, you can double up on Sean's gear. Does Danny have a rod and tackle?'

'She's outfitted,' Kyle said.

'I'll bring along insect repellent,' Andrew said. 'It might be necessary. All right — onward.'

The dogs ran ahead as they walked to the lake. They didn't follow the path to the dock but turned off along another pathway. It led to a rocky dock that they walked out onto. The dogs stayed behind, exploring the bush.

They set up the fishing gear on a flat rock that already felt hot from the sun. The picnic basket was placed under the shade of a tree.

'It's real deep here,' Sean said, wandering along the edge of the rock.

'Keep away from the edge,' Andrew told him. 'We don't want you falling in.'

'I can swim.'

'I know, but it's deep and cold, and the current's iffy.'

First Kyle and Sean dug for worms, then they gave Danny pointers on how to fix the worm to the line, then how to cast her rod. She knew, anyway, but let them have the satisfaction of teaching her.

'She's not bad,' Kyle said.

'Consider that a compliment,' Andrew

told her as he cast his line and it landed with a gentle ripple in the water.

While they fished, Danny and Andrew sipped cups of steaming coffee; the boys had cans of pop. Backing the boys' chatter was the wash of the lake against the rocks and the scuffling around and panting of the dogs.

'What we catch is supper tonight,' Andrew said, as if they needed incentive.

'Who's gonna cook?' Sean asked.

'I am,' Andrew said. 'You're all invited for dinner. We'll call your parents over.'

'Mom'll like that. She hates cooking.'

'No, she doesn't,' Sean said.

'Yes, she does,' Kyle argued. 'She's always saying she hates cooking.'

Andrew glanced at Danny. 'How're you doing?'

'Fine.' She had her back to a rock, her body in the shade. There was a pleasant breeze off the lake. Being with Andrew and the kids was like being in a family. It would be fun to be married to

Andrew, who was so competent with children. He treated the boys like equals, while keeping an eye out for childish exuberance, likely recalling his own boyhood and the pitfalls experienced.

After lunch, when the pail was filled with enough fish for dinner, the sun went behind the clouds and stayed there. Banks of darkness hovered over the other side of the lake.

Danny noticed Andrew watching the clouds.

'Rain?' she asked.

'Yep. It feels pretty stormy.'

'It does. Quite humid.'

'I think we should make tracks, boys,' Andrew said. 'Gather the stuff.'

The boys were quiet on the walk home, tired from their early morning and the fishing. The dogs flopped down on the porch.

'You don't have to bother with dinner,' Danny told Andrew.

'I promised,' he said. 'I'll give Doug and Carolyn a phone call. You guys can hang on here. I have work to do.'

Andrew phoned Doug and Carolyn, and they accepted the invitation. The boys and Danny joined the dogs on the porch. Danny sat in the rocking chair. Kyle and Sean settled down on an old couch, with Andrew's portable radio. Andrew took off in his truck.

He returned a few hours later to find everyone still stretched out on his porch, content. The weather was turning more ominous by the minute.

'We're going to have a doozer,' he said and gave the boys a wake-up call so they could help him clean the fish.

Carolyn and Doug walked over. Andrew cooked the fish in the oven in bread crumbs and served it with salad from his garden. They ate outside on the porch — real casual, sitting around chatting, waiting for the storm. But it didn't come.

The sky cleared again, the sun feeling hotter than ever. They all straggled over to the Cannons' house, Andrew carrying his towel and swim trunks rolled beneath his arm. Tonight everyone seemed tired, so their swim was sedate, with no raucous fun.

The boys, almost asleep on their feet, went to bed. The sky clouded over again, and when it began to rain, they had to scurry around and move themselves inside. Doug suggested that it was the perfect opportunity, with them all here and the boys in bed, to sit in the kitchen with Danny's tape recorder.

'You can count me out,' Andrew told them. 'I haven't got anything to say that I haven't already said.'

'I'm sure you have,' Danny said.

'No, I don't.'

'You're a spoilsport,' Carolyn said. 'You realize we're going to be mentioned in a magazine article. We can make a difference to someone who reads what we have to say.'

'She's right,' Danny coaxed. 'I'd like to have your permission to mention Drake Farm, to be able to quote what you said the other day about the food chain, about farms needing to be alive. A story about this farm will give a positive slant to my piece, and hope for America's farmers.'

'She's convincing,' Carolyn said.

'So was . . . ' Andrew sighed. 'Look, I'm tired. Another night, Danny.'

Doug placed his hand on Danny's arm. 'Settle for us tonight. Leave Andrew for a while. You have a few more days.'

'I suppose,' she said, disappointed.

'Andrew, are you going to walk back in the rain?' Carolyn asked.

'It's not too bad.'

'Here, Danny,' Doug said, fishing his truck keys off the hook, 'take him home. When you come back, we'll get to work.'

Danny had never driven a truck. She didn't tell anyone that, though. Carrying the keys, she rushed through the sprinkling rain with Andrew. When they were both in Doug's truck, she started the engine, relieved to find an automatic transmission.

On the way home Andrew was silent. So was she. What could she say that wouldn't precipitate some sort of argument?

He jumped out at his house. 'Thanks,' he said. 'It was a good day. See you.'

'See you,' she told him and didn't look back through the rearview mirror as she returned to Doug and Carolyn's.

As Danny hung the keys on the hook, Carolyn said, 'He's putting up his guard well and truly.'

'And you're not going to interfere,' Doug insisted. 'Danny won't be here very long. It's not fair to either of them to have you meddling in their affairs.'

'She's not meddling,' Danny said. 'If we wanted to fall in love, we'd fall in love.'

'Don't you want to?' Carolyn asked.

'Carolyn, leave it,' Doug said. 'Go get your recorder, Danny. We'll tell you what we know, although it's Andrew who can give you the little extra from his experiences as a child here.'

'I'll just have to do without his experiences,' Danny said and went to her room to fetch her tape recorder.

Danny sat up late, typing her notes into her computer, the rain on the window matching the clinking of her keys. She stored her data on a diskette labeled Sunflower Farm. Instinct told her the article was going to be easy to write because of her emotional reaction to the farm. And to Andrew.

Especially Andrew.

She shut down the computer and prepared to go to bed. She wouldn't be wrong, she thought, by saying they were definitely attracted to each other. *And that's putting it mildly, Danny. You like him too much for your own good. And if he does like you, then as Carolyn says, he's putting his guard up. So lay off him.*

Despite the overnight rain, the next day was hot and humid. Danny spent a lot of time in the pool with Carolyn and the boys. Doug returned to barbecue hamburgers and hot dogs in the

140

evening. No sign of Andrew. No one mentioned his name.

Monday was the same. Hot, humid, dripping with moisture. The sunflowers in the fields appeared weary.

'Storm brewing,' Doug said when he came home, and tossed his Stetson onto the hall table.

He was restless all evening. So was Carolyn.

'Storms can mean trouble,' she explained. 'Lots of crop damage.'

The phone beeped. Doug grabbed it. Andrew was standing by, waiting for trouble.

Danny went to bed, but she couldn't sleep. She got up and sat by the window, looking out at the still air. Sheet lightning flashed over the horizon and brightened the vast sky. Danny held her breath. She counted: One. Two. Three. Like she used to with Len when she was a kid and he was older, protective.

Thunder rumbled. More lightning, closer now. There was thunder all around. Danny jumped.

The wind picked up suddenly. Trees swayed, swished, tossed leaves. The rain came, pounding on the roof, waking the boys. She heard them call out, 'Mom!' She heard the phone and heard Doug speak. Andrew?

The storm was overhead now. Danny crawled into bed and tucked her head in the pillow, the comforter close to her neck. All they could do, she supposed, was wait it out.

She must have slept because she awoke to daylight, a door slamming, an engine revving.

Carolyn rapped on her bedroom door. 'Danny, are you awake?'

'Yes.'

'The guys need my help. I'm going with them. Can you give the boys breakfast?'

'Of course. Hang on.' Danny rushed out of bed and opened the door. 'Was there much damage?'

'That's what we're going to inspect. If you give the boys breakfast, you can all come and help because some of the flowers might need tying up. Wear jeans and a substantial shirt. If you need anything, check my closet. The key for the van is on the hook over the hall table. The boys know. Okay?'

'Okay. I hope the damage isn't too extensive.'

'We'll cross everything.'

A horn honked outside.

'Gotta go,' Carolyn said. 'See you later.'

Dressed in jeans and a long-sleeved blue shirt borrowed from Carolyn, Danny supervised the kitchen that morning. Luckily the boys sensed the emergency and cooperated. They wore jeans, shirts, boots, and their Twins caps. Danny put on hers as well. Kyle also suggested they pack some coffee and food in a basket.

'Good thinking,' Danny said. 'You know about these things. I don't.'

It was much cooler this morning — brighter, sunnier, the earth pure, sweet-smelling, like the fresh laundry the other day. As she drove with the kids, she didn't notice too much damage to the corn crops, but some of the beautiful flowers had been crushed. Some struggled valiantly to survive, reaching their faces to the sun, while others lay stretched out on the ground. Another field was untouched, all the flowers having their usual daily sunbath after a refreshing soaking the night before.

The boys told her where to drive around the farm to search for the others. They located them hammering in stakes and tying up rows of flowers. Danny parked the van beside the trucks at the edge of the field and tugged out the picnic basket. With the boys, she walked over to where they were working.

'She brought a snack,' Doug said. 'Good thinking.'

'Thank your sons,' Danny told him, putting the basket in a clearing. 'How's it going?'

'It's not too bad,' Carolyn said.

'Mainly two or three fields got bashed. And there's a tree down over by one of the cornfields.'

'Firewood,' Andrew put in, shifting his hat back on his head. He didn't wear his sunglasses today. 'I hope that coffee's hot.'

'I boiled the water,' Sean said.

'Then it's likely scalding.'

Everyone stopped for coffee and a sandwich. Then the boys, under the instruction of their father, began to help in the field. Carolyn showed Danny how to knock a stake into the rain-softened soil, run a string along, and prop up the plants that needed stabilizing. Andrew seemed to be avoiding her.

She knew she shouldn't be thinking about Andrew's behavior in an emergency situation, but it became so obvious he wasn't speaking to her, she felt a trifle embarrassed. Hopefully the others were too busy to notice.

They worked methodically through one field, then another. The sun grew hotter. Danny tugged the Twins cap to shade her eyes. Andrew wore his sunglasses now. She understood his need to be covered all the time.

When the fields of crops were shipshape, they checked the downed tree. Andrew and Doug used a chain saw on the fallen trunk and the branches while Danny, Carolyn, and the kids stacked the logs in the back of Andrew's pickup.

By late afternoon the picnic basket was empty. Danny had thought at the time that Kyle and Sean were overdoing the sandwiches and cans of pop, but now she realized they weren't.

'Feeling okay, Danny?' Doug asked.

'Fine, but the sun's hot.'

'Well, we're done. Not much damage, thank goodness.'

Danny heard his relief. Too much damage and their complete crop would be down the drain. She understood then how a farm could suddenly go broke. A few years of bad storms, droughts, no harvest, no income, and suddenly the farmer is in debt and there's no way out but to sell off the land or leave it ruined.

Danny drove the boys back to the house in the van; Doug, Carolyn, and Andrew followed in the trucks.

Andrew came onto the porch for a cold drink.

'Are you going to stay a bit, Andrew?' Carolyn asked.

'No. I'll head for home. I have to unload the wood. Thanks for all the help, everyone. Be seeing you.' His prowly walk took him to his truck. He opened the door and then turned around.

'Ah, Danny,' he said.

She looked at him. 'Yes.'

'I'll be getting the engine delivered tomorrow. Do you want to drop over about noon and see how it's going?'

'Sure,' she said. 'It means I might be able to leave soon, doesn't it?'

'The end of this week, all being well.'

Danny lowered her eyes. She didn't want him to see her sadness, because suddenly she didn't want to leave this place. *Ever*. 'That's wonderful,' she said. 'Thank you.'

'Thank me when you eventually drive away in your car.' He levered himself into his truck, slammed the door, waved, honked, and took off in a spatter of gravel.

She noticed that everyone had gone into the house. She joined them in the kitchen and drank another gallon of water.

'We've worn her out,' Carolyn said. 'Danny, for heaven's sake, take a shower or go dump yourself in the pool. You shouldn't have stayed out all day.'

'I wanted to help,' she insisted, removing the hat and fluffing her hair, which felt heavy from the heat.

'Sure you're fine?' Doug asked. 'We're used to being out in the sun all day.'

'I'm sure I'm fine,' She smiled. 'I'm just pleased the damage was minimal and you haven't lost your crop. But I will go for a swim.'

She gently floated in the pool, the weariness easing from her body. And she thought of Andrew — his golden tan and burnished hair and sinewy physique. How was she supposed to forget about blue eyes and a nice white smile? Forget that he lived alone in that big farmhouse with only his TV, VCR, CD player, dog, and cat for company, and that she wouldn't mind living there with him? Working together. Baking bread.

But she might as well not think about any of that because Andrew wouldn't let himself fall in love with another city woman.

The aroma of Doug's steamed fish in foil done on the barbecue drew Danny from the pool. After dinner she felt stronger, more confident. Andrew was going to begin fixing her car tomorrow. In a few days she might be on her way back to Buffalo.

★ ★ ★

Danny stayed up in her bedroom all the following morning to organize her research material for her article. She had some good stuff, but she still felt there was a sag in the middle. A sag that could be repaired by Andrew with a few stories about the family background of the farm, some of the early struggles. It would add an emotional texture to build up the loose facts she'd compiled. Without Andrew's complete input the article lost its fervor. Because Andrew was her main interest.

However, she knew how he felt about contributing to her piece, so she wasn't going to push him. She would just have to write brilliantly about what she had already learned.

She put on a clean white T-shirt with her denim shorts to go over to Andrew's at noon. She brushed her hair and even rubbed a little eye-shadow on her lids to highlight her eyes. She was downstairs when the phone rang. Realizing she was alone in the house, she picked it up, said 'Hello' formally, while uncapping the stick pen beside the pad, preparing to write down a message.

'Danny, it's Andrew.'

'You recognized my voice from a hello?'

'Carolyn always says her name, Doug grunts, and the kids scream. That being the case, I eliminated the Cannon family. Besides, I've talked to you on the phone before. Remember that first day?'

'I remember,' she said, thinking he seemed to have forgotten his silent mood of yesterday, unless he'd just been preoccupied, worried that his living had been crushed by the sleight hand of nature. Maybe it had nothing to do with her. Maybe he liked her but that was it. Possibly it was her own feelings that were all out of proportion. So she made her voice light. 'How're you doing?'

'Great. Ray Freeman, a friend of mine, delivered your engine this morning, and we've been working on your car. It looks good, and Ray's going to help me to quicken things up.'

'Wonderful. I don't know what I would have done without you, Andrew.'

'The service center would have done the engine work and charged you a pretty penny, I'm sure.'

'You're charging me as well.'

'We'll discuss that later. Are you coming over to see your car and meet Ray?'

'I was just on my way out. I'll be walking. Fifteen minutes.'

'Fine. See ya.'

It was hot, the sky pure blue, and the fields once more alive. Danny walked through the shortcut, enjoying the quietness with an intensity because soon she wouldn't have all this to enjoy.

When she reached Andrew's house, Sadie bounded up to her. Rolfe raced up a tree and peered at her cautiously from between the leaves. Warned of a guest by Sadie's bark, Andrew walked out of his garage, wiping his hands on a rag. A slim, dark-haired man about

Andrew's age followed him.

'Ray Freeman, Danny Murphy.'

'Hi,' Ray said shyly. 'Lovely car. Sure you don't want to sell?'

'Never,' Danny said.

'It was her brother's,' Andrew put in. 'He died.'

'That's too bad. Nice legacy, though.'

'If that's all I can have, yes.' Danny walked with the two men into the oily-smelling garage.

It was explained to her that they would lift her engine out on a hoist and replace it with another one. Easy.

Sure, she thought, looking at the size and weight of the engines. *Rather them than me.*

'Okay with you then?' Ray asked.

'Okay with me. I can't leave without the car, unless I leave it behind and take some other form of transportation home, which I don't want to do, obviously.'

They walked out into the sunshine again.

Ray said, 'Andrew told me you were

doing an article on this farm.'

'On Midwestern farms in general, but Drake Farm will take center stage as I know so much more about it.'

'Interesting,' Ray said. 'Andrew's got some stories, I'll bet.'

'I bet he has,' Danny agreed, giving Andrew a sideways glance. She almost told him that Andrew wasn't being cooperative but decided against putting in her two cents' worth. Why bother riling Andrew when he was helping her with her car? And why bother, anyway, when soon she wouldn't be here?

'Do you want to hang around and watch?' Andrew asked.

'No. I'll let you guys get on with it. Can I take Sadie for a walk to the lake for a swim?'

'Sure. Go ahead.' Andrew whistled, and Sadie came over, wagging her tail. 'Danny's taking you for a walk, Sadie girl. Lucky you.'

Lucky you? Did he mean that he wouldn't mind being taken for a walk by Danny? Or did he merely mean lucky Sadie? Danny tried not to think what he meant as she walked with Sadie at her side along the shady path to the lake.

She sat on the dock while Sadie swam and quickly ducked out the way when the dog shook.

'I know your tricks,' she told the dog, petting her damp coat. 'Come on. Let's return you to your master.'

Danny returned with Sadie, stopped for a pop break with the two men, and listened to their plans for the Trans Am's engine. It sounded complex and expensive. She hoped Andrew would charge her a fair price. He was losing time on the farm, and Ray's time was probably valuable as well.

After the pop break she lost the men's attention as they once more pored over the car. So she walked back to her cousin's. Countdown, she thought. A few more days here. Then home. But she knew home would never be the same again.

6

'Andrew's got Ray Freeman to help him with my car,' Danny told Carolyn, 'so I'll be leaving at the end of the week, or maybe on the weekend. I'll phone my editor and tell her. And I'll phone my sister as she's watching my house. I said I'd call her when I was on my way home so the family wouldn't be worried. They weren't sure of my schedule, anyway. Neither was I.'

'We're going to miss you,' Carolyn said. 'You will visit again, won't you?'

'Of course I will, and hopefully you'll visit me. Bring the boys to see Niagara Falls, and maybe we can go to New York City.'

'We'd love to, but you understand farming is a pretty full-time job, and our only time off is in winter.'

'Anytime's fine,' Danny assured her.

She began to pack a few of her

things, but she held off on the phone calls. She didn't know for sure when her car was to be ready. That event determined the day she would leave and eventually arrive home.

The sound of an engine made her stop what she was doing. After a moment Carolyn called upstairs. 'Danny, Andrew wants to speak to you.'

Danny ran downstairs and out the front door. 'I'm here.'

Andrew touched his hat, took off his sunglasses, and drew in a breath before he spoke. 'We're going to have a delay. We need some more parts, plus a special tool. It might be a few extra days before your car's fixed.'

'Oh,' she said, knowing she sounded disappointed. She was geared up to leave, emotionally and physically.

'Is it going to put you behind?'

'I might have to drive quicker,' she said. 'I have a deadline for this article, plus another one due a week after that.'

'I'm sorry.'

'It's not your fault. It's no one's fault.'

'We're dealing through the Pinedale Service Center, so even if they'd been doing the work, you'd have the same problems.'

'I'm not blaming you, Andrew.'

'I wish we could hurry things up for you. It's lousy, your having to hang around like this.'

'It's okay. I haven't alerted anyone I'm on my way home yet.'

'That's good news, I suppose. Are you getting bored?'

'Not at all.'

He shifted his booted feet. 'Do you want to come around and inspect the crops with me? To make sure all our hard work the other day was worth it.'

'I'd love to.'

'Great. Grab a hat. It's hot out there.'

Danny returned to the house and told Carolyn where she was going, and Carolyn gave her a tattered straw hat to wear.

'Glamorous,' Danny said, making a funny face.

'You look sweet. Have fun.'

Carolyn's pleased, Danny thought as she climbed in beside Andrew. *She wants a romance out of this. And she's going to get one if I don't leave here soon.*

It didn't help Danny's condition one bit as she spent the day following Andrew between rows of full-leafed corn, watching his slow smile, and sharing a chicken sandwich with him at lunch. Each time she was near him, brushed him accidentally, or spoke to him, her heartbeat increased and her pulse jumped.

After a while she jammed her straw hat low on her head, the way Andrew did his hat, and hoped he wouldn't see sheer longing in her expression. Maybe he pushed his low for the same reason, so no one would notice that he was hurt or lonely. But she'd noticed. And he'd touched her heart somehow, although why today, out of all days, she would suddenly have her feelings blossom into love, she didn't know. Possibly the emotion had been simmering all along. From the moment Andrew glanced through his rearview mirror and gave her that funny sensation in her stomach, she was likely doomed, tossed onto a roller coaster with no escape.

'You are feeling okay, aren't you, Danny?' Andrew asked.

'Yes. Do I look pale or something?'

Andrew smiled. 'A little weary perhaps.'

'You stride fast.'

'Well, we're finished now. Let's return to the truck. We can put our feet up for a second.'

He walked close by her side to the truck and opened the passenger door for her, and she slipped onto the seat. He came around to his side and sat with his knees raised on either side of the steering wheel. Danny stretched out her own legs.

'This tape recorder thing,' he said.

'Will it take long?'

'Depends on how many stories you want to tell.' Danny's heart raced. Andrew was capitulating. Wonderful! She'd have her article research complete to take home.

'When do you want to do it?' he asked.

'Whenever you're free.'

'I'm free tomorrow. Come for lunch, bring your gear, and we'll talk.'

'Thanks, Andrew.'

'I guess I was being a little gritty about it all.'

'I won't say anything harmful,' she promised. 'Really, I won't. Everything that has happened here to me has been positive. Everything I write will be positive.'

He turned to look at her, eyes behind his dark glasses, cap low. He reached out and tipped the brim of her straw hat. Surprised by his action, Danny's heart skipped a beat. She couldn't see his expression, but his touch on the hat felt gentle and caring.

'You're a good kid,' he said in a soft voice.

Then he shifted his legs, started the truck, and drove up the road.

Danny leaned back against the headrest and closed her eyes, replaying Andrew's tipping the brim of the straw hat over and over.

During the evening Danny kept her excitement over the interview down. She didn't tell Carolyn or Doug that she finally was having her interview with Andrew. She wanted her time with him to be special, just between them.

The next day she packed her canvas tote with tape recorder and notebook and walked to his house. When Sadie barked, he came out on the porch, wearing his looser jeans and a crisp blue-check shirt.

His casual clothes, Danny thought, walking up the steps. Was he dressed up for her? The hat incident made her think he was. Were they falling in love with each other? Is this what love was?

A slight thickening of the throat? A need to have him smile at her? A need to be allowed to touch him? A need for him to touch her? Did he feel the same way?

'How's it going with the car?' she asked as she followed him through the house into the kitchen, as she had that first morning. It seemed so long ago now, as if she'd been here forever. As if she'd known Andrew forever.

'Ray's picking up the last missing part Friday morning. We'll work on it Friday. All being well, you should have it Saturday or Sunday.'

'Then I can leave?'

'Yes. You can leave.'

Danny felt like weeping when she saw the lunch, because he'd gone to some trouble. He'd cut up fresh salads into little wooden bowls, to be eaten with slices of his warmed bread and butter. Coffee was ready in a silver percolator. There were also oatmeal cookies. The meal was laid out on the kitchen table on willow-green place mats. There was a vase of wildflowers in the center of the table.

'This looks lovely, Andrew,' she told him, sitting down when he pulled out a kitchen chair for her.

'Thank you,' he said, pouring her coffee before he claimed his own chair. 'Shall we eat before we talk?'

'Yes. Otherwise the tape will likely be garbled.'

He smiled. Danny smiled. They smiled a lot.

They didn't speak much. Love . . . was it silent? Did you just know?

When they were finished eating, they went into Andrew's cozy living room and sat on the couch. She put her tape recorder on the coffee table.

'I'm not good at talking into these things,' he said.

'Pretend it's not here.'

'I'll pretend I'm talking to you.'

'You are,' she said.

'I know.' Then he smiled.

He lost his self-consciousness as he warmed to his subject and explained to her about topsoil erosion. The reason he kept fields uncultivated during the winter months was so he wouldn't lose precious soil to wind. He recorded memories of his childhood, the hopes and dreams of his parents, and his plans for the future of his farm.

Danny knew she should be feeling ecstatic while he spoke, because she was finally getting the information she wanted. But she didn't. In a few days she was leaving this man behind. Sometime in the future she might see Doug again, and he would tell her that Andrew was married or having children. He wouldn't be lonely anymore. And she would say to her cousin, how nice for Andrew. But how miserable for herself.

She closed her notebook, turned off the tape, and said, 'That's great, Andrew. Really great. Thank you so much.'

'You got what you came for. You're quite wily. You know how to get around people.'

'Nothing intentional about that,' Danny said.

'Probably not. I suppose you're just a nice woman.'

'And you're a nice man.' She stood up and packed away her tape recorder and her notebook, zipping her bag over her precious cargo. Andrew's voice. Then she turned around.

She knew in that second Andrew was going to kiss her. She didn't want that. Well, she did want it, but she knew if he kissed her, then the feelings they were harboring between them would be exposed. Once exposed, Andrew, she sensed, would become serious. And so would she. Who was she kidding? Then she would hurt him when she finally drove away from his farm.

She stepped away, removing herself from his outstretched arm. 'Carolyn's expecting me back,' she said softly.

Sadness. Disappointment. She saw the feelings cross his face. *It's better this way, Andrew. Believe me.*

He thrust his hands into his jeans hip

pockets. 'Do you want me to drive you over?'

'I can walk.'

'It's real hot. Come on.'

Danny followed him from the house to the truck. He opened the passenger door for her, and she climbed in. He came in beside her and shooed Sadie away. Poor Sadie. She sat by the house, tail wagging forlornly as Andrew backed up and drove away.

To Danny's surprise he kept going past Carolyn and Doug's house. 'We've been thrown together for almost two weeks now.'

'That's the problem — thrown together, Carolyn trying to match-make.'

'I'm feeling stuff, Danny, and I don't like it. I don't want to feel stuff for you. I've been this route before. And she said she loved me and wanted to marry me. And then she up and left because she realized she couldn't live here.'

'I think I could live here,' Danny said, 'but my life is at home.'

'*Think. But.* Negative words.'

'We barely know each other,' she said.

'Yes, but you can tell, can't you, when it's happening?'

Danny rubbed her bottom lip with her tongue and gazed out the window at the beautiful sunflowers they were passing. Fields of gold, heads turned to the sun, happy.

'You're lonely,' she said. 'Any woman would do.'

'That's not true. Aren't you lonely?'

She looked at him. 'I have a fulfilling life. I have two sisters, my nieces and nephews. I have my parents, friends, my business acquaintances. I've lived all my life in Buffalo. I own my own home. Well, I don't own it, but I pay a mortgage instead of rent.'

'Do you have a boyfriend?'

'No.'

'But you like city life?'

'Yes, I suppose. I've never really experienced anything different.'

'You see, you might think you like it

here at the moment, Danny, but down the road, when it's thirty below in the winter and the wind's howling around the house, you'll wonder where you're at.'

He stopped the truck at a dead end, backed it up into a turnaround, and began to drive back toward the houses.

'Is that what happened with Lise?' she asked.

'Carolyn tell you who she was?'

'Just her name.'

'What happened was, she was in town living with a girlfriend she went to college with and working at a bank in Pinedale. We met at one of the dances. And fell in love. She said she'd marry me, and we began to make plans. Then one day she said she wanted to stall the plans for a while; she had to go back to Boston. When she returned to Boston, she wrote me, calling everything off.'

Danny lifted her hand and touched Andrew's on the steering wheel. 'She hurt you badly.'

'Yep.'

'I wouldn't do that, Andrew. I might like you a lot, but I'm not going to lead you on, especially as I'm unsure about things, about how I feel.'

'I wouldn't let you lead me on,' he said as he halted the truck outside the Cannon home. 'I might be lonely, but it hasn't affected my brain. I'm not going to do anything with you. We've had a nice time. When it comes to your leaving, we'll say good-bye, adios, and that'll be it.'

Danny withdrew her hand. 'I'm pleased you feel that way. We're even.' She opened the truck door and gathered her bag. 'Thanks for the lunch, the interview, and the ride home.'

'You really got what you came for.'

'I never expected to end up here. With you,' she said. 'I didn't come to Minnesota to see you. You happened to be here. An opportunity, if you like. But if you think an interview is more important to me than you as a person, then you' — her voice faltered — 'you can think again, Andrew.' She slipped from her seat, put the strap of the tote over her shoulder, and closed the truck door, fighting tears.

'Danny,' he called.

She turned to look at him through the open window.

'I'll call you when your car's ready.'

'Thank you,' she said.

As she walked around the house toward the screams and splashes she heard coming from the pool, she didn't look back. What was the use?

Carolyn saw Danny as she came around the house. 'Isn't Andrew with you?'

'He went home.' Danny put down the bag and slipped out of her shoes as she joined Carolyn on the patio. She sat down in a plastic lawn chair.

'I saw Andrew's truck go barreling by a while ago. Were you with him?'

'Yes. We were talking.' Danny pushed back her hair, trying to make room for some breeze on her heated skin. It wasn't fair. Why fall in love with a man who lived thousands of miles from her own home?

'You sound serious,' Carolyn said. 'Have you gotten serious with him? Do you want to discuss it?'

Danny stared at the pool. Kyle and Sean were quiet for a moment, dangling their feet from perches on the edge. 'It can't be,' she said, 'and that's that. There's nothing to discuss.'

'Sure?'

'Sure.' She smiled at Carolyn. 'I've just had a great time here, Caro. My car will be ready Saturday or Sunday. I guess I'll leave first thing on Monday. That way I'll be home in the week for the following weekend. I'll have time to get my article written then.'

'Did Andrew come across the way you wanted him to?'

'Yes. He talked about his mom and dad, how they inherited the farm from his father's father, his grandfather. He showed me some photos. He still hasn't really come to terms with his father's death, has he?'

'No. They were pretty much a twosome since his mother died when he was fifteen. Andrew hasn't had it easy. Tough emotionally. I don't think it was all Lise's fault they broke up. Oh, she might have returned to Boston, but I also feel that she didn't think she could love him as much as he needs to be loved. Get me?'

Danny nodded. 'Got you.'

'But I think you could. You have the capacity, something that Lise didn't have. You wouldn't be frightened off.'

'I'm not sure, though, Carolyn. It's been sudden. It might just be the summer, this place. You know how it is — anywhere away from home is better. The grass is greener and all that. My memories might not be as intense as the real thing.'

'So you'd have to go home to know?'

Danny nodded. 'To know for sure. Because I couldn't hurt Andrew again, not the same way.'

'I understand that.'

'And also, Carolyn, he might have a

thing about women from out of town, because it can't be permanent.'

'You might be right. He's pretty self-sufficient, isn't he? He might not want a woman in the house, really.'

'He might enjoy being lonely. Maybe he's masochistic.' Danny laughed. 'Good excuses, anyway. How did you know when you were in love with Doug?'

'I walked into Pinedale High on the first day of a school year. It was a frosty morning, and we were still wearing summer clothes, so I was shivery. I went, 'Ooh,' and Doug was near me. He grinned and said, 'Talkin' to me?' I said, 'Not really, but you'll do. It's chilly this morning.' He said, 'Let me warm you up. I'll take you to the movies on Friday night.' The rest is history.'

'You never broke up once?'

Carolyn shook her head. 'Not once the connection was made.'

That's what she couldn't do, Danny thought — make the connection with Andrew.

7

'I've just come by Andrew's place,' Doug said on Saturday afternoon, 'and your car is running, Danny. Is it ever! That's one powerful engine. Hike over and look. He's expecting you.'

Danny should have been joyous. Her feet should have lifted from the ground as she walked. Instead, they felt like lead. She didn't want to leave, but she had to. There hadn't been any connection made with Andrew, not something permanent. Like a kiss. Or words: *I love you. Stay here. Come back to me.*

The Trans Am's engine rumbled. Sadie came barking and leaping at her.

Ray's face beamed from the driver's seat.

Andrew grinned. 'We did it,' he said when he saw Danny. 'It's better than ever.'

'Listen to that roar,' Ray said and

turned off the ignition. He left the car.

'Thanks, guys,' she told them. 'I owe you both. I owe everyone. Where's a good place for dinner? Someplace fancy. Sunday evening.'

'You don't have to, Danny,' Andrew said.

'Carolyn, Doug, the kids, all of you. I do have to.'

'O'Bannon's maybe,' Ray suggested. 'Good food, dressy atmosphere.'

'Where is it?'

'On the highway, the other side of Pinedale,' Andrew told her.

'I'll book for us all. Ray as well.'

'Ah,' Ray said.

'If you're not there,' Danny warned, 'I'll come searching for you.'

'She's tenacious, so believe that,' Andrew said.

Danny smiled at him, and he smiled back. She felt her heart leap. Did his heart leap?

'So are we going to test-drive this heap?' Ray patted the side of the Trans Am.

'Sure we are,' Andrew said. 'Danny, you want to drive or — '

'You drive,' she told him, because she knew he wanted to. He was itching to get his hands on the steering wheel, his foot on the gas pedal.

'If I clean up first, you can drive me home,' Ray said. 'My brother dropped me off this morning, so I have to rely on a drive, anyway.'

'Good thinking,' Andrew said.

Ray went inside the house to wash.

'I'd better do the same.' Andrew disappeared after Ray.

Danny ran her hand over the hood of the red car. 'Well, Len,' she said, 'your car's been fixed with love and adoration, that's for sure.'

Ray came out first and shyly smiled, but didn't speak as they waited for Andrew. Andrew wore a clean white shirt with his jeans. He let Ray into the small backseat and slipped into the driver's seat. Danny sat next to Andrew and fastened her seat belt, holding her breath, hoping the test run would be perfect. For the guys' sakes, for all their hard work, not for her sake. She didn't want to leave; her heart felt really heavy.

Andrew turned the key, the engine started, and he drove cautiously from the farm, down the dusty road to the place where she'd broken down. He turned onto the highway, away from Pinedale.

'Ray lives this way,' he explained. 'His dad has a farm.'

'You work the farm?' Danny asked, looking back at Ray.

'Two brothers, father, mother, and sister,' he said. 'All farmers.'

'Ray has cattle,' Andrew put in. 'A dairy farm.'

'Interesting. Is it running well?'

'For heaven's sake, Danny, let it go,' Andrew snapped.

Danny saw Ray's eyes question his attitude.

'It's okay,' she said to Ray. 'I'm not going to mention your farm in the article. I have what I came for.' She almost glared at Andrew but didn't.

After all, he'd fixed her car. Maybe he did it because he wanted to make sure she left.

Danny didn't speak the rest of the way to Ray's place, which was quite a long drive. Instead, she stared out at fields that stretched to meet the sky.

The Freemans' farm was a messier place than Andrew's. Farm machinery lay dead in fields. Mud caked the cattle barns. Ray's family home was white clapboard with a few straggling sunflowers and black-eyed Susans trying to survive.

'Thanks,' Ray said as he left them in the car. 'Good luck, Danny.'

'Thank you very much for your help,' she told him. 'And Andrew will call you to let you know the time for dinner on Sunday evening.'

'That'll be nice. See you then.'

Andrew drove away from the house, saying, 'I didn't mean to be abrupt earlier, Danny, but I didn't want to get into the Freemans' farm. They've had some hard times. His dad hasn't been well. Lots of heavy medical bills.'

'I noticed the difference in appearance between his farm and yours,' Danny said. 'I'm sorry if I spoke out of turn. But if that's the case, shouldn't he be paid for helping you?'

'I paid him.'

'*You* paid him? I'm supposed to pay him. I'll pay you back.'

'I don't want anything from you. I won't be a charity case. I can afford the time and the engine.'

'You won't be a charity case? I don't see the reasoning in that. You work, you get paid for it. It's the way it is, no charity involved. But by pandering to your pride, you're making me indebted to you, Andrew. Do you realize that?'

'Get off your high horse, Danny. It's difficult enough as it is.'

'What's difficult?'

'You. Me. You know.'

'Can't we be friends?'

He glanced at her, his eyes hidden behind his sunglasses. 'It doesn't work that way. Lise said that — let's be friends. I can't be friends. It's all or nothing.'

Danny turned sideways in the car. Her hair blew in the wind — she couldn't call it a breeze — from the open windows. 'What are you saying?'

'That I like you. Too much.'

'I like you as well,' she said, all her caution lost. 'Really like you, Andrew.'

He drove past the entrances to his farm, heading toward Pinedale. 'Let's go on a date — a real date, not something organized by Carolyn.'

'They're expecting me home.'

'We'll stop and phone.'

Danny straightened in her seat. The car moved smoothly along the highway. Andrew looked at home driving it, as if he were made for the car, as if her car were his. And vice versa. As if they were made for each other, interchangeable.

'The car runs well,' she said. 'It's great.'

'You'll have no trouble going home.'

'I'll have trouble,' she admitted, 'leaving you.'

'You don't have to go.'

'Yes, I do. I have commitments. I also have to know for sure.'

'Do you believe in love at first sight?'

'I don't know.'

'When I saw you standing beside this car that day, I felt it was inevitable.'

'Don't, Andrew. It might not be. I might get home and never return or never see you again. I had a friend who went to Arizona after college. We promised to write, to phone, to visit. We never did. She's married now and has one kid, and I heard that through another friend.'

Andrew drove into Pinedale and stopped at one of the fast-food outlets. 'I'll phone for you,' he said, leaving the car. 'What do you want to eat?'

'I don't think I can eat.'

'Root beer?'

'Love one.'

The sun burned hot through the windshield. Danny sat, not thinking. She didn't want to think. If she thought, her brain might explode.

Andrew returned with two drinks. He passed one to Danny through the window. The plastic cup was filled with ice and felt cold against her hands.

He got in beside her and rested his own cup on the dashboard.

'Carolyn said stay out as long as you want. No rush home. She wasn't having anything special to eat tonight, anyway.'

'She'd say that, anyway,' Danny said, sipping the drink. 'I haven't had root beer in an age.'

'I always have it when I come here. Best and only root beer in town.'

Danny smiled. 'My sisters are older than I. They tell stories of going out on dates to drive-ins, and all they ever had were burgers and root beer.'

'Great American invention.'

'Sure is, although we're both supposed to be into organic.'

Andrew lifted his leg and perched his booted foot beside the floor shift. 'I can go organic for so long, and then hunger sets in.'

'So you pig out and undo all the good?'

'It does *me* good,' he said, and he removed his sunglasses. He hooked them over the steering wheel and picked up his drink.

His eyes were such a deep blue, Danny had to glance away. It was almost as if he were acting persuasive. Or was this just how Andrew was on a date? Nice, friendly, devastatingly handsome. No wonder Rosemary Smith had been chasing him since high school. If she felt the way Danny did about Andrew, the poor woman must be in agony.

'Well, you certainly don't put on weight,' she said.

'Neither do you, little Danny. You're small.'

'Five-four.'

'Really?'

'You're tall. Over six feet, aren't you?'

'Six one, last measurement. My dad used to be over six feet. When he got old and sick, he shrunk.' Andrew sighed. 'That's another movie, isn't it?'

'You can talk about him with me if you want.'

'Not on a date. On a date we should have fun. Finished your drink? We'll go driving.'

'Where do you want to go?' he asked as they backed out of their parking spot and drove toward the exit.

'Take me to O'Bannon's. We can book for Sunday.'

'That's an idea. You think, Danny.'

Danny liked O'Bannon's. It was a small restaurant, set in nice gardens. The menu looked interesting, and they took her credit card. She booked for everyone under her name while Andrew waited by her side.

But the act of booking the meal seemed like a last ritual. Monday she would leave. She had to. She had no choice.

Back in the car, Andrew headed toward town. 'There's not much to do on dates here except drive.'

'I like driving, especially along these

empty highways. The traffic at home can get gruesome.'

'Sometimes you don't sound as if you like it there.'

'I like it.' Danny reached over and punched on the radio. Pop music blared from the station she'd been tuned to all those days ago.

'We sometimes drive up to the Canadian border. Do you want to do that?'

'Whatever you do on dates here, I want to do,' she said.

So they continued driving, the sun baking them, the wind roaring in their ears, drowning out the music, until Andrew turned the volume higher.

Crazy, Danny thought. *Here I am, my second to last night, with the man I could love if I gave myself half a chance. Driving — plain old driving, and I'm having a ball, a wonderful time. I don't want to be anywhere ever again but here with him.*

The border was only a small crossing. 'Nothing much,' Andrew said.

'It looks the same on the other side as it does on this side.'

'Flat fields.'

Danny laughed. 'When we go over the border, we leave one freeway for another and drive to Toronto. Another city.'

'As I said, not much around here.'

Andrew reversed the car, and they began the homeward drive. And as they drove, the sky clouded over. Forked lightning was seen over the fields. Droplets of rain, like the imprints of dogs' paws, settled on the windshield. They wound the windows up. The sky was a range of color from red to purple to black. Gilt edged the clouds. Thunder rumbled a long way off. The radio crackled.

Andrew sighed restlessly.

'Worried about the farm?'

'No. I don't think this is anywhere near us at home.'

'Shouldn't we go home to check?'

'Yes, we should. And we're on our way.'

'Our date's over.'

'I suppose,' he said.

Andrew's mood had changed. Danny sat silent, not wanting to talk about how much they liked each other and why they couldn't be together, or if it was love.

She was quite relieved when he turned into Drake Farm. It hadn't rained here, but the clouds from the stormy air lingered above. He turned toward his house.

'I didn't feed you dinner,' he said.

'I don't need anything,' she told him. 'I've eaten well since I've been here. I've probably gained pounds.'

He stopped the car. 'Are you taking the car home to Carolyn and Doug's?'

'Why not?'

'No reason. It's fixed. Runs well, doesn't it?'

'Excellent.'

He slid his arm along the seats, and his fingers touched her hair. He stroked a couple of strands over her shoulder, which was bare because she wore only a tank top.

Danny saw his breathing quicken. She felt stranded between his hand and his eyes. Then he leaned forward and placed his lips upon hers. Gently, barely a kiss, more a whisper.

When he straightened, he dropped his hand to the seat. 'It's too bad,' he said. 'But I appreciate your honesty.'

I love you, Andrew, was her impulsive gesture, but she couldn't say the words. What if she returned home and found, like Lise, that her life was truly not here?

8

Danny made her phone calls on Sunday morning to her family to tell them she would begin traveling on Monday morning. She didn't confirm the actual day of arrival, because that depended on her driving stamina.

After that she packed, leaving out her denim shorts and a clean T-shirt for driving in, and her pink dress and sandals for the dinner at O'Bannon's. She wished she had a fresh dress to wear for Andrew, but as she didn't, the dress would have to do a second time.

She also packed up her computer and her tape recorder. She was going to be busy when she got home, with not much time to think or remember. Except she couldn't forget the touch of Andrew's lips against hers. She wanted it again before she left, to remind her how it felt to fall in love in Minnesota in a sunflower summer.

Of course, Andrew would soon be busy with the harvesting. Doug said this morning at breakfast that the seeds were just about ripe. Andrew wouldn't have much time to sit around remembering, either.

She went downstairs and out to her car for her map. She'd planned on maybe going home through Canada, but she didn't really have time to sightsee.

When she walked into the kitchen with her map in hand, Carolyn remarked, 'It looks like you're really going now.'

'Well, I am,' Danny said. 'I have to plan my route.'

'I want you to phone each evening when you reach a motel. You have to be careful, Danny. I keep thinking how lucky you were to come across Andrew when your car broke down.'

'*I* think I'm lucky Andrew happened along. Out here you could wait for days before another truck ventured by.'

'That's true. We're miles from any-where.' Carolyn joined Danny at the kitchen table. 'So which way are you going home?'

Danny spread her map over the table, located where she was, and placed her fingertip on the map. 'Over to Duluth, through Wisconsin, and across the Mackinac Bridge. That way I don't have to go around Chicago. Then down past Detroit, Cleveland, and around Lake Erie to Buffalo.'

'It doesn't look too far.'

'Try driving it sometime,' Danny said. 'It's three days at least.'

'Take it easy. Don't tire yourself out. I wish you were going to have company.'

'I'm fine. I'm used to being alone. Single and twenty-six, you do a lot of things alone.'

'I suppose that's true. Never having been single at twenty-six, I don't know much about that. I went straight from home to Doug.'

'A babe in arms,' Doug said, joining

them. 'What's this, Danny? Planning your route?'

She nodded.

'Car in good shape?'

'Better than it ever was, likely,' Danny told him. She leaned her elbows on the map on the table. 'You know, guys, Andrew won't take any payment; he paid Ray himself. Even taking you all to O'Bannon's doesn't repay him or you.'

'We don't need repaying,' Doug insisted. 'We're family, Danny. You didn't even have to take us out, but we won't say no. I fancy a juicy medium-rare steak. O'Bannon's makes 'em the best.'

'It'll be nice to all go out, anyway,' Carolyn put in. 'But as far as paying Andrew . . . if he doesn't want anything, he doesn't want it.'

'He'd say that even if he were broke,' Danny said.

'True,' Doug agreed. 'Andrew's pride can sometimes be a source of frustration. But don't push him. If you really want to pay him, send him a check from home.'

'Would he cash it?'

'Depends on how he feels that day, I suppose,' Carolyn said. 'Andrew gets my goat sometimes.'

Danny smiled. She was going to miss Carolyn terribly. And Doug, who was so much like Len.

In the afternoon she drove her car to Pinedale. She kept the windows open, reminding herself of the freshness of the air, the way it tossed her hair, and how she was going to miss it.

When she pulled up at the pumps in the Pinedale Service Center to gas up, the young man who came out to help her said, 'Is this the car Andrew Drake fixed?'

'Yes, it is.'

'Running good now?'

'Excellent. Thanks for your help.'

'We only ordered the new engine.' The guy leaned back to check the pump to see how much gas he'd put into her car. He gave her a price, and

Danny handed him her credit card.

'A new engine?' she said.

'That's right. Nothing but the best — Andrew insisted. We could have gotten him a reconditioned one quicker.'

'I see,' Danny said and waited for her credit card to be returned. She signed the bill. 'Thank you.'

'Have a good trip.'

'I will.'

A new engine.

Danny drove on into Pinedale. She went past the high school, up the street she'd shopped with Carolyn where she'd bought the rose-pink dress, past the old movie house where the dance had been held. She drove farther, on to O'Bannon's, where they were going tonight. She parked, walked inside, checked the reservations, and eliminated the two boys from the list. Kyle and Sean had something on, so they couldn't come. Danny promised to leave money with their parents to take them for a burger and shake later.

Danny returned to her car, wondering why Andrew had put a new engine in her car, when she was sure he'd told her specifically it was reconditioned. And why did he make her wait for the new one when a reconditioned one would have been quicker coming and could have been installed earlier? Had he wanted her around longer, or was he just being nice? Because Andrew was nice. Kind. Considerate. Thoughtful. Careful.

Tears burned Danny's eyes as she drove back up the highway toward Drake Farm. Tonight . . . leaving Andrew . . . was going to be one of the most difficult events of her life to date.

She didn't eat the rest of the day, wanting to save what little appetite she had for the restaurant meal this evening. When it came time, she dressed in her rose-pink dress, adding a silver rose pin to one strap, leaving her throat bare. On impulse she upswept her hair, clipping it with a silver fastener. She had rose earrings to match the pin.

Now I look more like a city woman, she thought as she checked her reflection.

Even though it was a tight-fit rear seat, Doug and Carolyn wanted a ride in the Trans Am, so Danny elected to drive to O'Bannon's. That way it was her entire treat. Ray was meeting them at the door. She stopped to pick Andrew up.

He wore a light gray suit, blue shirt, and darker tie. As he fastened the belt of the passenger seat, he nodded to Danny. 'Nice evening.'

'It sure is. Not so hot tonight.' How strained she sounded!

Carolyn leaned over and felt Andrew's shoulder. 'Did you get that suit out of mothballs?'

'No,' he said, turning around with a smile. 'I bought it when I went to Pauline and Frank's wedding.'

'I remember now,' Carolyn said. 'Pauline and Frank are cousins of

Andrew's,' she added for Danny's benefit.

'So you do have family around here?' Danny asked.

'They're in Minneapolis,' Andrew answered. 'Not really around here.'

Danny drove along the gravel road and out onto the highway. It was the first time she'd driven with Andrew beside her, and it felt strange. She felt him watching her hands on the steering wheel, the way she checked her rearview mirror, just the way she drove in general. Len had taught her to drive — taught her how to drive into a skid in the icy parking lot of K-Mart, how to drive in heavy snow, and how not to spin her tires. She was a pretty good driver. She could change the oil, but she didn't know what Andrew knew about engines.

'I'm in the right direction, aren't I?' she asked anyone in general. She didn't want them to know that she'd driven into Pinedale this afternoon. She wasn't going to say anything to Andrew about the new engine. To do so might embarrass him, expose his reasons when in the end she was leaving, anyway.

Doug said, 'Yeah, just keep going, drive through town, out the other side.'

'She knows what the place looks like. We went there the other night to book,' Andrew told him.

'The night you didn't buy your date dinner,' Carolyn reminded him.

'I offered a burger with the root beer.'

'I didn't want anything,' Danny said. But she thought, *I was too choked up, too thrilled, too happy to be with Andrew to think of eating.*

'My wife wouldn't understand that,' Doug said. 'Carolyn never, and I emphasize *never*, passes up food, especially free food.'

'Doug,' Carolyn protested, 'you make me sound like a pig.'

'You broke me when we were in high school. I spent all my allowance on you.'

'I never liked my mother's cooking,

so if you said you'd take me for a burger, I'd go.'

'I hope you didn't tell your mother that.'

'Once in a while,' Carolyn admitted.

'Then no wonder your parents wanted to get away from you. Having you for a daughter is embarrassing.'

'Beast,' Carolyn said, and in the rearview mirror Danny saw them lean toward each other and kiss. Their lips lingered.

Danny and Andrew glanced at each other, looked away, and looked again.

'Your hair's nice, up like that,' Andrew said. 'Very sophisticated. It makes you look much older. Are you sure it's not getting blown around by the open window?'

'No. It's fine and easy to repair,' she said. 'You look nice in a suit, more sophisticated.'

'Do you wish I were more sophisticated?'

'Don't start, Andrew.'

He reached out, touched the dash,

and glanced downward, as if he couldn't take much more.

And neither can I, Danny thought. *Just tonight, and it's all over.*

Ray was waiting by the restaurant door, dressed in slacks and a sports jacket. They all went into the cool interior of the restaurant together. Danny gave her name, and they were shown to an alcove table where they could overlook the flower garden.

'This is nice,' Carolyn said.

Danny was seated next to Andrew, with Ray on her other side and Doug and Carolyn opposite.

'Okay, folks,' Danny said, 'it's carte blanche. All on me.'

'That means we can have anything we want,' Andrew said.

Danny gave him a look. But underneath the tablecloth she felt his fingers grope for hers. He squeezed her hand. Tears filled her eyes. She tugged her hand from his and reached for the menu.

The meals were well prepared but

very wholesome. Meat, potatoes, and vegetables. Desserts of homemade pie and ice cream or creamy cheesecake. Everyone, including Danny, felt stuffed afterward. She paid the bill, and they walked outside into the warm evening.

'Really great, Danny,' Ray said before he went to his truck. 'Thank you very much.'

'Thank *you* very much,' she told him, squeezing his arm. 'I really appreciate your help on the car.'

Ray's face was pink after her squeeze. Danny figured he didn't go out with many women, as he was awkward and shy. 'It's okay,' he said. 'Anytime. Safe trip.'

'I will. Thanks.'

They walked over to the Trans Am while Ray took off from the parking lot.

Danny handed her keys to Andrew. 'Have a last drive,' she offered.

He took the keys from her, his hand touching hers.

On the way home Danny couldn't join in as the others discussed the meal and how good it had been. She was leaving. This was it. Tonight. Tomorrow she would never travel this highway again to Pinedale, never sit beside Andrew in a vehicle, never see him again.

When Andrew parked outside his house, Doug and Caroline said they were going to walk home.

They disappeared quickly, leaving Andrew and Danny alone, standing by her car. Ready to say good-bye?

'Come inside,' Andrew said.

Danny followed him up the porch steps, taking one last look at the red-and-blue handwoven rug on the floor, the rocking chair with the stars-and-stripes knitted blanket. She listened to the way the screen door twanged and Sadie barked — black and white with liquid eyes, adoring her master, tolerant now of her master's visitor.

Andrew let Sadie outdoors and closed the front door. 'Want something?' he asked.

Danny touched her stomach. 'No, thanks.'

'It was a good meal, Danny. A pleasant end to . . . ' He averted his glance from her and took off his suit jacket, loosened his tie, and began to roll up the sleeves of his crisp dress shirt.

'I'd better go,' she said. 'I have a long drive tomorrow. I need sleep.' She smiled. 'Beauty sleep.'

He stretched out his hand and let the back of it flutter down her neck, trail over her shoulder. 'You don't need beauty sleep. You're so naturally pretty.'

'I don't want to leave, Andrew; you know that. I've explained that I have to.'

He put his arms around her. 'Please — to remember you by.'

Danny wrapped her arms around him and rested her head on his chest. He felt strong, safe, secure.

'Let's walk down to the lake while it's still light,' he said softly.

'Let's,' she whispered.

They released each other. Andrew

brushed his fingers through his hair; Danny wiped traces of tears from her eyes.

They left the house quietly by the back door, but Sadie heard them, anyway, and met them at the path.

'Come on,' Andrew said, his voice sounding husky.

'She won't be left behind. She loves you.'

'She likes you as well.' Sadie ran ahead of Andrew. 'She doesn't let anyone take her for a walk or a swim.'

'I feel honored, but I never really got around Rolfe.'

'Rolfe was my father's cat. Even I can't get too close to him, but once in a while he'll roll on his back and let me rub his stomach.'

'Panda and Thunder are so used to the kids, you can do anything with those two cats.' Danny knew they were filling in space with their words. The sensible part of her wanted to say good-bye right away and leave, while the irrational part wanted to draw out her time with Andrew way into the night.

Sunflower Lake looked like a mirror beneath the evening sun. Shadows from trees and rocks lay on the surface. They walked up the dock, Sadie ahead of them.

'No swimming, no shaking,' Andrew warned Sadie. 'We're in our best clothes.'

Danny didn't think she'd ever wear the rose-pink dress again. What did it matter if Sadie shook spray on it?

Andrew stepped slightly ahead of her, hands in his pockets, his arms bronzed beneath the rolled-up shirtsleeves. He moved his broad shoulders as if he had a load on them he wanted to shrug off. Danny wanted to touch his hair, to feel his lips upon hers pressing hard, just for a minute, a second.

'Andrew,' she said softly.

He turned and she walked into arms. His lips were warm and firm, his arms a haven. Danny let her fingers stray into his hair. Silky. Sungolden. She held him to her for the last time. Or was it the first time?

Then he let her go, and she walked back down the dock toward the path. She ran, her feet almost catching a tree root and making her tumble, but she righted herself. At his house she hurried around the side and opened the door to her car. Andrew had left the keys in the ignition. Her small white purse was on the passenger seat. She started the engine, backed out, and with gravel flying took off to Carolyn and Doug's.

As she neared their house, she realized she couldn't face them in this state. Tears streamed down her cheeks, making them feel puffy. So she drove on past their house, taking a road between sunflower fields. When she felt she was far enough away from everyone, she stopped the car. And, sitting in between two fields of smiling sunflowers, she had a good cry.

9

Danny respected Carolyn and Doug for their restraint when she returned to their house. They didn't question her red eyes or what might have transpired between Andrew and herself. All Carolyn said was, 'Have a good night's sleep, Danny; then you'll be fresh for driving.'

When I leave here, I'll be fine, she told herself as she packed the rest of her things and zipped one of her bags. She felt like leaving the rosepink dress in Carolyn's spare-room closet, but realized that would only upset Carolyn. Besides, it needed a wash and press. Danny would do that when she arrived home before putting it away for good. The dress would act as the symbol of her time here in Minnesota. Her memories of Andrew were tied up in that dress. And each and every time she saw a sunflower in a garden or field, she would think of Andrew.

She didn't sleep very well, and if she'd been in a motel alone, she would have left early. But she had Carolyn and Doug to think of, to say good-bye to. That was another difficult moment waiting for her.

In the morning, as she dressed and packed the remainder of her gear, she decided that she wasn't the perfect candidate for vacations. She got too involved in the places she visited, and they became a nostalgic memory that ended up on that shelf of life's what-if's. She was better off just staying home and doing her work.

She sat down at the table by the window where she'd done her computer work and wrote a check to Carolyn. It wasn't to cover her expenses for her stay, because she knew Carolyn and Doug would be offended if she thought she owed them any financial recompense. It was to go to some farm-aid cause, if there was one. If she couldn't pay Andrew or Ray directly, at least she could help in a roundabout way.

Ready to leave, she carried her bags downstairs, packed them in her car, then returned to clear the room of her canvas tote and the check. She left the check with a note in the kitchen, not wanting Carolyn to turn it down.

'Are you leaving already?' Carolyn asked. 'Have some breakfast . . . a last coffee with me.'

'Okay. Outside by the pool.'

'I'll call Doug.'

They drank their coffee, talked about nothing in particular. How could you talk particulars when you weren't going to be here tomorrow or the next day? Danny thought. She hugged the boys, Doug, and Carolyn. Everyone had tears in their eyes. She was pleased they liked her enough to show that much emotion.

She climbed into her car, opened the glove compartment, and took out the sunglasses she wore for driving — an old pair of mirrored ones of Len's. They hid her expression, her eyes, her tears.

'Phone tonight,' Carolyn insisted. 'And write. And visit again.'

'I will,' she said. 'Thanks for everything.'

Then she was backing the car and waving. The dust from the road floated around the car as she drove off. She slowed by Andrew's house and turned in. His truck was gone. She sat in her car, gazing at the house. New white siding. Brick-red shingles. Pink and white hollyhocks. Sunflowers still begging to be let in on the party.

Where was Andrew? She wanted to see him once more — a quick glance from a distance.

She drove and found his truck parked beside a field. A black-and-white speck — that was Sadie. A man in jeans, checked shirt, green John Deere hat. And fields of golden-yellow sunflowers, their round mahogany faces soaking up the bright sun, stretching to the blue horizon.

''Bye, Andrew,' she said and drove away, wondering if he'd seen her.

It was sweltering hot driving on the highway. The pavement was soft and oozed the odor of tar. More than once Danny wished the car were air-conditioned and longed for a dip in Carolyn's pool. She stopped for lunch in an air-conditioned restaurant. She drove on, stopped for dinner, drove on again. She booked a cabin on the shore of Lake Superior and walked on the beach, where she threw some rocks. Then she phoned Carolyn, who sounded distant, not in voice but in time. Danny was gradually moving farther away, closer to her own life. But for a while she'd been let into someone else's.

She arrived home Wednesday afternoon and parked in front of her garage. Before unpacking her car, she opened up her house. Despite her sister's presence — mail piled on the kitchen table, a pink plastic watering can on the counter for the ritual of weekly plant care, and a bunch of written messages in Susan's round writing — the townhouse felt unused. After being closed up for a month, it smelled of the peach-color paint on the walls and her cozy tweed sofa bed and leather armchair.

She opened all the windows upstairs and downstairs to let in what she could of a breeze from the humid heat. Then she unloaded her car and took her bags to her bedroom. She transferred her portable computer to her office. She also had a desk computer.

Unsure quite what to do first, she phoned around to her family, all of whom were pleased to hear from her and glad to know she was safely home. Her parents invited her for dinner the following evening. Susan had some extra messages and told her to check out her answering machine.

Danny did that, then showered, changed into navy slacks and a pale blue T-shirt, and made a list of groceries she would need for the following week.

She locked up the house once more, drove to the market, and shopped. She was not used to pushing a grocery cart around a store and decided vacations stripped a person of routine.

Having had a decent lunch, Danny snacked on a sandwich for dinner and watched TV, something she hadn't done the entire time at Carolyn and Doug's even though the kids had it going incessantly. Then she went out into her square of garden. She weeded and watered her flowers, thinking she should get some sunflowers to brighten up her fence on one side.

I'm not thinking about Andrew, she told herself when it was dark and she was indoors undressing for bed. Tomorrow she would begin her article. And then another. And another. It wouldn't take long to be back to her routine.

Except she hadn't bargained on the memories while she wrote the article. Nonfiction was supposed to be fact, not emotion, she thought, but that wasn't true. She liked to put emotion into everything and add characters. Readers related to people stories. Were writers supposed to cry as they wrote?

Hoping for a break, she drove over to her parents' house for dinner. They lived in a nice middle-class neighborhood, with lots of shade trees and split-level houses with swimming pools. As they ate in the spacious dining room overlooking the backyard, Danny told her mom and dad all about her trip. About the car breaking down, about Andrew helping her. She rushed over that bit. Mainly she dwelled on Doug and Carolyn and the kids. Her mother was delighted and said she would write to them all right away to renew contact.

Her friend Anne came over the next evening. They ordered take-out Chinese to eat on Danny's patio. Anne, a petite blonde, unmarried like Danny, worked as a fashion buyer in a department store. She was always on the lookout for a husband and wanted to know if Danny had met anyone.

Danny mentioned Andrew. She had

to talk to someone about him. And why not Anne, who had been her friend since kindergarten?

'Do you think it would work?' Anne asked as she spread egg rolls, chicken fried rice, strips of beef with broccoli, and deep-fried shrimps with lemon on the patio table between their chairs. 'Dig in.'

Danny picked up a plate and filled it with portions of food. 'How could it work? He's a farmer. He can't move.'

'But you could?'

'Yes, I could.'

'Do *you* want to? That's the question. Or didn't he ask you to stay?'

Danny speared a shrimp with her fork. 'He mentioned staying, but I wasn't sure. He can't be hurt again.'

'You're so magnanimous, Dan. What about *you*?'

'I'll get over him. Put him in my memory bank.'

'And that's what you want?'

'He never said he loved me. He'd always be thinking I was going to leave.

It wouldn't be a good relationship.'

'It sounds wonderful to me,' Anne said. 'I'd move for a guy. Anything to get out of a rut.'

A rut? Was she in one? Not necessarily. She enjoyed her work. The article spewed from her brain, through her fingers on the keys, to the computer screen like magic. It printed smoothly, and she hardly had to change a word. Neither did Gina, her editor.

Gina phoned and said, 'If you can keep this up, I'll raise your rate. It'll be out next month. I'll send advance copies. And Andrew Drake sounds just gorgeous. Was he?'

'Gorgeous,' Danny said.

Sungold.

But after that article, nothing else would come. She felt numb, brain-dead. She decided to get out and about. She went for picnics by Lake Erie beaches with her sister and her kids. She accompanied her single sister, Rita, to Rochester, where Rita had a business meeting. They drove in Rita's BMW and stayed at a ritzy hotel.

And summer was quickly receding. Even September looked a little like October this year. Leaf color changed early. First frost was almost upon them in Minnesota, so the harvest would almost be over. What did Andrew do in winter? Was he as lonely as she felt?

Danny had never felt lonely before, but now she did. If she let herself, she would actually mope around. And then the advance copies of *Earth Now* arrived in her mailbox. She read her article, and it made her cry again. She addressed manila envelopes, one to Carolyn and Doug, and one to Andrew. She took the envelopes to the post office, stuck on stamps, and placed them in the mailbox. *Hope you like it, guys,* she thought as she drove home.

10

'Danny, you're so quiet,' her dad said at dinner one evening when she joined her family at her parents' house.

Sue, Tony, and the kids were there. Plus Rita, in between business meetings. All were seated around the heavy oak table, the place they'd sat for family gatherings all their lives.

'I'm just sleepy,' Danny said. 'It's the cool weather after the heat of summer.'

'The heat of summer dispersed nearly two months ago,' Sue pointed out. 'You've been different since you came back from that Minnesota trip.'

'It was meeting all your mother's family. It must have been a shock,' her father said.

Danny's mother gave her husband a look. 'My family is very nice. They were nice, weren't they, Danny?'

Danny smiled. 'Very nice.'

'So nice, in fact, she wants to give everything up and go and live there. Isn't that the case?' Rita asked.

'No,' Danny said.

'Well, something happened,' Sue chimed in. 'Did you meet a guy? Only men make women stupid.'

Her husband, Tony, groaned.

'It's the truth,' Sue said. 'Did you meet a man, Danny?'

Danny didn't have to answer. Rita, sharp, clicked her fingers in the air. 'I know. The guy who fixed her car. The farmer.'

'Don't say farmer in that tone,' Danny said. 'Andrew would not like it.'

'Andrew. Is that the guy?'

'The man who fixed my car. Yes.'

'Did you have a hot romance with him?'

'Of course not.'

'But she fell in love with him,' Susan said. 'Didn't you, Dan?'

Danny had to admit it someday. If she didn't, she was going to burst with the emotion, the feelings that left her longing, aching for Andrew. 'Yes. I fell in love with him. But I had to come home. I wasn't sure then. Really sure, that is. He didn't want to help me with my article on the Midwest farms, but he went along with it eventually. I sent him a copy of the article over three weeks ago, but I haven't heard from him.'

Her mother patted her shoulder. 'Oh, dear.'

'Fly out and see him,' Rita urged. 'I'd do that.'

'I'd rather he came to me,' Danny said. 'He's been hurt before by a woman from Boston. She went home, never went back. He has to learn that he can trust me. And I don't even know if he loves me.'

And I might never know, Danny thought as she arrived home later. She checked her mailbox even though it was Sunday. She checked her mailbox more than most people, anyway, hoping for acceptances, checks for her articles, rejections for ideas. Now she was waiting for a word from Andrew. And if no word ever came, then, she supposed, he didn't care about her.

Her friend Anne said that she'd rent the town house from Danny if Danny went to Minnesota to live. That way Danny didn't have to sell her property, and Anne would have a better place to live in than the apartment she shared with a friend now. Danny liked that idea.

To keep herself from falling apart, she jogged an extra quarter mile each morning along the paths behind her place. She swam at the indoor pool close to home. She sent out a few ideas for articles, ideas that had been around for a long time, nothing new she came up with. Gina asked for a follow-up article to the one in Minnesota.

★ ★ ★

Autumn turned everything golden, reminding Danny, as if she needed reminding, of Andrew's hair. Outside her window, the sky was blue like his eyes. The sun glared on her computer screen. She turned the monitor this way and that on the swivel stand, trying to focus. She had a document made up. *Earth Now: follow-up article on Minnesota farms.* Eastern farms? Eastern farms in winter? She could take a trip to New Hampshire. Vermont? The colors were beautiful in those states in the fall. Maybe she'd meet another man, someone who would take her mind off Andrew.

The phone rang. She ignored it, thinking she had her answering machine turned on. Obviously it wasn't. The phone kept ringing.

She gave up and moved her chair on its casters across the rug to the desk beside her computer desk.

'Danny? It's Carolyn calling.'

Danny's heart raced. She could barely speak. 'Carolyn, it's good to hear from you!'

'We had some mix-up in the post office. Anyway, we've only just received the copy of your magazine. The article was super. Really super. We're nuts about it. Doug's showing everyone in Pinedale right now.'

'Did Andrew get his?'

'Yes. He's impressed, Danny. So impressed that . . . He wanted this to be a surprise, but I don't think you should be surprised. He's driving to Buffalo. I don't know when he'll be there, but I'm telling you to expect him. I hope you don't mind.'

'Mind? No, I don't mind.' No pretense now. She was too far gone. 'Do you know when he'll be here?'

'Not exactly. He took off a couple of days ago. We've got Sadie, and we're feeding Rolfe. Something in the article set him off. He said he had to see you.'

'I can't wait to see him. I've decided I can work from anywhere. My friend wants to rent my townhouse.'

'Then you're ready if he's serious?'

'If it happens. Yes.'

'That's good, Danny. I think you two

are a great couple. Let me know how it goes.'

'Will do.'

Danny hung up the phone, stood up from her chair, and danced around her office. Andrew was driving here to see her. Wonderful!

His arrival time was a different question. A day passed; no word from Andrew. Another morning passed; no word from Andrew. Danny shut down her computer after lunch. She couldn't work.

She prepared a carafe of coffee, changed into navy slacks and a blue-and-white sweater so she'd look nice in case he arrived. Then she waited. Brushed her hair. Waited. Brushed her hair. And waited.

It happened all at once. The Cannons' maroon minivan was outside her house. Carolyn didn't mention he'd borrowed it. Andrew got out. He wore jeans, a sweater, and a black leather jacket. He checked a piece of paper against the number on her house and walked up the driveway. Danny held her breath.

The doorbell rang. She ran to answer it. She wanted to throw herself in his arms, but all they did was smile at each other.

'Hi,' he said.

'Hi. Come on in.'

'You don't seem surprised I'm here.'

'Guess who phoned.'

'I knew she would. She didn't think I should just barge in on you.'

'She doesn't want you hurt, that's why.'

'I can take care of myself. Sometimes we have to take risks, don't we?'

'Yes. Come in.' Danny ushered him into the narrow hallway and closed the door.

He stood, still holding the piece of paper. 'Your address,' he said. 'I ripped it off your envelope. Your article was something else. Really effective. Passionate.'

'Have some coffee. I made coffee not long ago. I measured your time and the distance and figured — '

'I'd be here today?'

'Yes,' she said and walked into the tiny kitchen, thinking how small it was compared to the country kitchens Andrew was used to.

'Let me take your jacket, Andrew.'

'It's fine. I'll toss it over a chair. I bought it on the way here. Do you like it?'

'Yes. Black suits you. Sit down.'

He sat down, looking long and lean in her home. A stranger? No, not a stranger. Familiar. Dear. Then why weren't they in each other's arms? Because there were things to talk about first. Because neither of them was absolutely sure about the other.

Danny poured two mugs of coffee and put one in front of Andrew. She tugged out another chair and sat down with her own coffee mug. 'You look different here,' she said.

He cupped his hands around her mug as if he were holding her . . . gently. 'So do you. I never saw you in anything but summer clothes.'

'I never saw you in a sweater, either. Is it cold there now?'

'We had some frost. Now it's Indian summer. It's pretty here.'

'The trees are nice. I should take you through a park.'

'I'll stay a few days. I booked into a hotel not far from here.' He sipped the coffee. 'This is good. Can you come out to dinner with me? A real date. A city date.'

'Oh, yes.'

'We'll talk then. Because I have some things to say — some things I learned about myself with you this summer. And since you've gone. And on the drive here.'

'I want to hear them,' she said.

After their coffee she showed him around her house. He liked her office, the view over the roofs, her little garden. He took a bundle of magazines she'd written articles for to read in the hotel room. When he left, he gave her the hotel name and phone number and said he'd pick her up again in three hours. She could choose the restaurant.

Unfortunately, it was too chilly to wear the rose-pink dress, which had been dry-cleaned and was covered in plastic in her closet. Instead, she chose a pink blouse, a burgundy skirt, and high heels. A city girl dressing up for her country beau? No. A woman dressing up for the man she loved.

Andrew phoned her from the hotel to say he was leaving. He drove up to her house on time in the van. Now wearing a suit, he walked up her driveway. She opened the door, touched his arm, tugged him inside her house and closed the door. He leaned over and kissed her. Their lips parted . . . retreated. Later.

He stroked down her arm with his palm. 'You look lovely.'

She closed her eyes for a second then opened them. He was still looking at her. His eyes were as blue as his shirt and tie. Was his hair longer? More golden? Or was he the same, and just better in person than in memory?

'I need a jacket,' she said and reached for a black blazer.

He helped her on with it, smoothing the shoulders.

They walked out to the van together. Danny directed him to a restaurant. Anne had taken her there for her birthday. The food was good, wholesome, and there was lots of it. Andrew ate big portions.

'It feels strange being in the van,' Danny said. 'I mean, being in the van here, not there.'

'We're mixing life-styles now,' he said. 'You know, if I'd visited Boston with Lise, things might have worked out. It's the unknown that is scary. Knowing where you live, seeing you here' — he glanced at her — 'you're no different.'

'Of course I'm not. And neither are you. You're not out of place. Besides, if we . . . I mean, if we get together, we'd have to visit here. My family is here. You'll have to meet them. Do you want to meet them?'

'Sure. Whenever it's convenient.'

'They'll drop anything to meet you, don't worry. And it happens to be a time when Rita, my high-flying career-oriented sister, is in town.'

'She sounds daunting.'

'She isn't, really, not when you know her. And Sue, my other sister, has three children. She's a bit like Carolyn. Not to look at, because Sue's taller, but down-to-earth, incorrigible.'

'And your mom and dad?'

'Nice, kind. They'll like you. You'll like them.'

'I'll have a family?'

'Yes.'

They ordered salads and chicken wings, the restaurant's specialty. Sharing the wings was fun, something to talk about, laugh over, be together over. How Danny had missed him! How she loved being with him! Anywhere. It didn't matter where. As long as she was with him.

She directed him to a park by Lake

Erie after dinner. They sat in the van and watched the dark water, lights twinkling on shore.

'I've been hard on myself,' Andrew said, resting his arms on the steering wheel. 'I tried to deny falling in love with you because I'm frightened of being hurt. It really wasn't much to do with Lise, after all. I realized that when you left. I tried to put up barriers — your article, for instance — to stop myself from liking you. I'd gotten over Lise ages ago. I tried to rationalize with myself about why I didn't fall for the hometown women, because that would be easy, wouldn't it? I'd have no excuse to let them go, to be sorry for myself.' He turned to look at her. 'I love you, Danny.'

She reached out and touched his cheek. 'I love you too, Andrew. I tried not to. I really wasn't sure when I left, either. I didn't want to hurt you again. Now I'm sure.'

He started the engine, drove her home, walked her to her door.

'Do you want to come in?'

'No,' he said. 'I want to treasure these moments with you. I want us to be really sure. I want to be as sure as you are.'

His kiss was light on her lips, but she could still feel it as she heard the van leave the curb. She had his phone number at the hotel. She knew where he was. She slept easy.

The next day she took Andrew to meet her parents. Her mother was extremely interested that he was Doug's partner. Since Danny had met Doug and his family, her mother was longing to meet them as well.

That evening he met Sue, Danny's nieces and nephews, Tony, and Rita. Danny thought Andrew found them overwhelming, but if he could handle Carolyn, he could handle her own sisters.

They spent the next days sight-seeing. They visited Niagara Falls. They drove into the New York countryside and ate at an old farmhouse restaurant.

They walked in the country, in parks, beside the lake. They shopped at malls where Andrew bought himself new clothes and gifts for the Cannon family. Intrigued by a fancy pet store, he also purchased toys for all the pets. And he bought Danny a diamond engagement ring. A small one, nothing ostentatious, a ring to join them together on their journey to becoming a couple.

'I think,' Danny said when they were at her place one evening, 'we'll get married in Pinedale. That way my mother can meet her family and we don't have to travel home after.'

'Is it going to be difficult for you to move?'

'No. I'll take what I want with me, and Anne will look after the rest here. I'll pick up anything else on trips home. All I have to do is drive carefully so my computer will be safe.'

'You're going to drive?'

'You want the Trans Am in the family, don't you?'

'Of course.'

Danny fluttered her lashes. 'Especially now that it'll last forever with its *new* engine.'

Andrew's cheeks flushed. Danny stroked the warmth with her fingertips. 'You shouldn't have done that.'

'How did you find out?'

'It's not because I'm an expert on engines,' she said. 'I went to gas up at Pinedale Service Center the afternoon before we went to O'Bannon's, and the guy told me.'

'No one in that town can keep their mouth shut,' Andrew said. 'I suppose you were mad?'

'Not really. Although, while it's nice to know I have a brand-new engine, I do feel I should have paid for it myself.'

'A new one was really expensive, Danny.'

'I do have money.'

'I know, but . . . It wasn't done intentionally to keep you there longer. If anything, I wanted you to leave. It was done because . . . the car, Danny, had to be saved. It was your brother's. I don't know. I felt it was very precious to you.'

'Oh, Andrew, it *is* very precious to me.'

'Now it'll last for a long time.'

'That's so sweet of you. And all that time we were fighting with ourselves, weren't we?'

'Yes, we were. But not anymore. Will you write about me again?'

'All the time. My husband the farmer, this. My husband the farmer, that.'

He laughed and put his arms around her and hugged her. 'I love you, Danny. I love you. I really do. And I'm really sure.'

She hugged him. 'I am too.'

He looked at her. 'I wonder why we were lucky and fell in love.'

'The magic of the sunflowers,' she said. And they kissed.

We do hope that you have enjoyed reading this large print book.

Did you know that all of our titles are available for purchase?

We publish a wide range of high quality large print books including:
Romances, Mysteries, Classics General Fiction Non Fiction and Westerns

Special interest titles available in large print are:
The Little Oxford Dictionary Music Book, Song Book Hymn Book, Service Book

Also available from us courtesy of Oxford University Press:
Young Readers' Dictionary (large print edition) Young Readers' Thesaurus (large print edition)

For further information or a free brochure, please contact us at:
Ulverscroft Large Print Books Ltd., The Green, Bradgate Road, Anstey, Leicester, LE7 7FU, England. Tel: (00 44) **0116 236 4325 Fax:** (00 44) **0116 234 0205**

SUMMER IN HANOVER SQUARE

Charlotte Grey

The impoverished Margaret Lambart is suddenly flung into all the glitter of the Season in Regency London. Suspected by her godmother's nephew, the influential Marquis St. George, of being merely a common adventuress, she has, nevertheless, a brilliant success, and attracts the attentions of the young Duke of Oxford. However, when the Marquis discovers that Margaret is far from wanting a husband he finds he has to revise his estimate of her true worth.

CONFLICT OF HEARTS

Gillian Kaye

Somerset, at the end of World War I: Daniel Holley, unhappily married to an ailing wife and father of four grown-up children, is attracted to beautiful schoolteacher Harriet Bray, but he knows his love is hopeless. Daniel's only daughter, Amy, who dreams of becoming a milliner and is caught up in her love for young bank clerk John Tottle, looks on as the drama of Daniel and Harriet's fate and happiness gradually unfolds.